"Could [barcode obscures text] ed.
"Maybe [barcode obscures text] nt, grab-a-bite after work, but an intentioned time with you."

"You see me most Sundays," Evelyn countered.

"I want to spend more time getting to know you apart from my family. When you're at our house, you spend your time with my mother. Don't get me wrong. That's wonderful. I love watching you probe your relationship with God. But I'd like to spend more time like we had this weekend. Alone. Getting to know each other."

She put a finger on his lips, stopping the words he intended to say.

"Don't say it, unless you mean it. Words are too easy to have meaning without action."

He stared into her eyes, their gray color picking up the hint of purple in the dusky sky. "If my words aren't enough, I don't know what else I can offer."

He opened her car door but stopped her before she climbed in. Mark took Evelyn's face in his hands and placed his forehead on hers. "I would never do anything to hurt you."

Her eyes searched his, measuring his words. She licked her lips. "Those are just words, Mark."

Words? Then he'd act. He lowered his lips and claimed hers in a kiss. Evelyn stiffened a moment then relaxed. He held her smooth cheeks lightly with his hands, then started to pull back, when a honk caused him to jerk away from Evelyn.

Her eyes stayed closed a moment before she opened them and slid into the passenger seat. Mark pulled the car onto the highway, a soft silence between them.

CARA C. PUTMAN lives in Indiana with her husband and three children. She's an attorney, lecturer at a Big Ten University, and involved at her church. She has loved reading and writing from a young age and now realizes it was all training for writing books. An honors graduate of the University of Nebraska and George Mason University School of Law, Cara loves bringing history to life. Her first book, *Canteen Dreams*, won the 2008 Book of the Year for short historical category. Cara regularly guest blogs at C.R.A.F.T.I.E. Ladies of Suspense and Writer Interrupted, as well as writing at her blog The Law, Books & Life. To learn more about her other books and the stories behind the series, be sure to visit her at www.caraputman.com.

Books by Cara C. Putman

HEARTSONG PRESENTS
HP771—Canteen Dreams
HP799—Sandhill Dreams
HP819—Captive Dreams
HP856—A Promise Kept

A Promise Born

Cara C. Putman

Heartsong Presents

Writing books is an endeavor that happens in solitude, but I have been blessed from the beginning with friends who stepped alongside me, believing I could do this and praying for me. To all my friends at Bethel Christian Life Center: Thank you for always encouraging me.

And many thanks to Stephanie Wetli, who asked if she could try editing a book. You didn't know what you were getting into, but your insightful comments have been a blessing. Thanks also to Sue Lyzenga for reading as it scrolled off the printer. I have the world's best neighbors!

And to Jesus: Thank You for looking across time and choosing to offer Your life as the ultimate sacrifice for my sin.

A note from the Author:
I love to hear from my readers! You may correspond with me by writing:

Cara C. Putman
Author Relations
PO Box 721
Uhrichsville, OH 44683

ISBN 978-1-60260-677-7

A PROMISE BORN

All scripture quotations are taken from the King James Version of the Bible.

Our mission is to publish and distribute inspirational products offering exceptional value and biblical encouragement to the masses.

PRINTED IN THE U.S.A.

one

May 1943

The grinding of brakes straining to bring trains to a stop vied with the final *whoosh* of steam. Even in the early evening, people hustled around the Washington DC Union Station. They darted between the trains lining the tracks, reflecting the excitement filling Evelyn Happ. She didn't know which way to look next other than down the tracks that led to her future. In moments, she'd join sixty-nine other Women Accepted for Voluntary Emergency Service, the navy's WAVES, as they boarded a train leaving Evelyn's home in DC for points west.

The WAVES would get off the train at an unknown destination, assigned to a job contributing to the war effort. That's all she knew. The cloak-and-dagger atmosphere only added to the sense of adventure. Her instructions mirrored that of the other WAVES: Board the B&O's Diplomat. Nothing more. Somewhere down the tracks, they'd get off.

The heels of hundreds of shoes clacked against the cement. Finally, the adventure had begun.

"Come on, Vivian." Evelyn grabbed her friend Vivian Grable by the arm. The waifish girl double-timed to keep pace with Evelyn's strides. "If you don't start moving, you'll miss the train."

"All the activity is fun to watch."

Lonnie Smuthers smacked her gum and rolled her eyes. "Don't push the girl, E. If you walk any faster, you won't need a train. I prefer to ride."

"Why won't the navy tell us where we're going?" Vivian brushed a strand of blond hair out of her cornflower blue eyes.

5

"War secrets." Evelyn grinned. "Don't worry, Viv. I'll stick close." Sometimes she felt bland compared to these two women. Neither her brunette hair, cut to the government-specified length and curling under her cap, nor her gray eyes stood out in the sea of WAVES.

Viv shook her head. "Fine. Let's get this journey underway. I'm ready for whatever the navy throws our way."

"It's why we joined." Evelyn pulled Vivian down the platform. "Adventure. Service. Intrigue."

WAVES service would be a vast improvement over anything Evelyn had found on the East Coast in the private sector. Few companies had taken her engineering degree seriously. All those hours working through textbook after textbook, studying and cramming didn't amount to anything without someone letting her do the work. She could have traveled to the West Coast and tried a company like Boeing, but she hadn't felt quite that adventurous. Somehow it was easier to head into the unknown in the company of a group of women she had trained with for weeks. Unexpected friendships had developed among them. Friendships that would make the coming unknowns an adventure.

The WAVES: smart uniforms, flexible navy rules. Most of all, the WAVES had a place for her to do something for her country. If she was really lucky, she would get to use some of that until-now-ignored education.

A whistle sliced the air, and Evelyn covered her ears as gals squealed around her. Soldiers hurried past them, all rushing to reach their trains. "There it is." Viv pointed with her free hand to track eight. "Let's hurry."

"Don't worry. We'll make it." Even as Evelyn said the words, excitement quickened her steps. She spotted the Baltimore & Ohio behemoth. The engine's gold lettering stood out against the black paint as it belched smoke. "Ladies, I do believe it's impatient to get us on board."

Lonnie groaned. "I highly doubt that mass of steel has a solitary feeling." She nudged Evelyn. "Get those romantic notions out of your head and climb aboard."

Lonnie's down-to-earth approach wouldn't weigh Evelyn down. No, she had the opportunity to do something meaningful with everything she'd learned while studying at Purdue University.

Finding the dark green passenger cars of the Diplomat, the gals climbed on board. Evelyn led the way down the narrow hallway until she found their sleeper berth. The three women crashed into each other and the walls in the small room until they'd tucked their bags out of the way. Other WAVES boarded, their excited voices fading as they found their berths. Moments later, a jolt shimmied through the train. Evelyn placed a hand over her stomach to stem the excitement. Sometime soon—the navy hadn't given any indication how far they would travel—she'd learn her role.

"We should try to get some sleep, gals." Lonnie pulled her hair into a net and washed her face. "Who knows what the morning holds?"

Evelyn might not know, but she could imagine. As she settled onto the top berth, she let her mind wander through the possibilities. Communications? Aviation? Code breaking? Evelyn doubted the navy would use her in the medical or Judge Advocate General areas because of her training. Regardless, the Allies needed all the help they could get, especially as the Battle of the Atlantic refused to go their way.

"I hope we're not going all the way to California." Viv's soft voice pierced the darkness.

Evelyn had to agree with Viv. She could only imagine how long it would take with the starts and stops to take on fuel and drop off passengers and mail. The suspense about her assignment might kill her during the journey. "Think of the beaches and sunshine. They wouldn't be so bad."

"How's a girl to sleep with all this jostling?" Lonnie growled from a lower berth.

The train threw Evelyn against the wall as it raced around a curve. She rubbed her elbow that had smacked the side.

"Carefully, though most people find it soothing, don't they?"

Viv nodded. "Relax into the berth."

"We could tie you in place, Lonnie." Evelyn kept her tone innocent. She shifted around until she found a comfortable position on her bunk. Evelyn pulled the thin blanket to her chin and forced her muscles to relax. Soon enough, they'd know their destination. She closed her eyes and surrendered to sleep.

❧

Too soon, sunlight filtered through the small window, and the conductor came through, banging on the doors. "Breakfast served for forty-five minutes."

Evelyn scrambled to get ready then hurried off while Viv and Lonnie started to dress. Women in sharp WAVES uniforms filled the dining car when Evelyn reached it. She took in the cacophony of voices as they anticipated their destination. Evelyn settled into the only open seat at a small table. "Morning, girls."

Quiet greetings answered hers. The gals at her table were familiar, though she couldn't remember their names. "Any idea where we're headed?"

A dark-haired beauty shook her head, a gleam of adventure in her gaze. "No, but I can't wait to learn our destination."

"Me, either." Evelyn leaned forward, ready to ask more questions, when a whistle cut through the noise. She looked to the front of the car.

"Ladies." Lt. Nancy Meyers swayed gently with the train. "Head back to your sleepers and pack. We change trains at the next stop. The conductor tells me you have fifteen minutes."

Evelyn grabbed coffee and rolls for Viv and Lonnie and hurried back to their berth.

She watched the scenery out the dirty window as her roommates ate their breakfast. Get off? Here? While the thought of getting off the train appealed, she hoped the final destination wasn't nearby. The flat land had been planted for crops and looked entirely rural. She fidgeted at the thought of being stationed near here, though a train change could still send them in many directions. Maybe north or south. Ten minutes later, the train slowed. Lt. Meyers knocked on their door. "Ladies, prepare to disembark."

Energy poured through Evelyn. This was it. Around her, women straightened uniforms and collected personal items. Vivian looked out the window. "We can't have gone far."

"My guess is Ohio." Lonnie shrugged and went back to packing.

Evelyn licked her lips. "Do they have cities in Ohio?"

Vivian laughed. "Sure, but it doesn't matter. If the navy says that's where we're going, that's it." Evelyn kept her knees bent so she could stand throughout the jolts and brakes of the train. The rural landscape had turned to city landscape. Maybe this wouldn't be so bad after all. She saw the sign alongside the tracks: CINCINNATI.

Later that afternoon, after a delay in Cincinnati and a short train ride, Evelyn looked around Dayton's Union Station. This one looked nothing like the one in Washington DC.

Dayton.

She let the name roll around a minute.

"Do they have any bodies of water in Dayton? We are in the navy, after all." She couldn't imagine any place so rural hosting a navy project.

"I'm pretty sure there's not even a coast." Viv shrugged.

Lonnie laughed. "It's as landlocked as a state can be."

Evelyn considered the facts. "Well, I can't wait to learn why the navy thinks we need to be here."

&

Mark Miller hunched over the plans spread across the table. He ran his fingers through his hair but didn't see anything different. The Bombe should work. Yet each time they ran a code, something happened. The machine refused to operate as designed.

Joe Desch, the wiry man leading the top-secret project,

stood at the head of the room and crossed his arms. "The navy wanted this machine operational months ago. What are we missing, gentlemen?"

The engineers filling the room slumped in defeat. They'd all worked too many hours for too many weeks to endure more dead ends.

"All right." Desch rubbed his chin. "We'll review this again tomorrow. Let's give Adam another test run."

Mark followed the group back to the sweltering room that housed the large computer. It might be a cool May day outside, but the machine raised the temperature to July levels in Building 26. Mark stared at Adam. Would the machine decode the German messages this time or break down in a flash of sparks? Each failure prolonged the stranglehold the Germans had on Atlantic transportation lanes.

The engineers had worked eighty hours a week more often than not since the National Cash Register Company had landed the navy contract to develop the machine. Mark had worked on the project since last September, employed by the brilliant Joe Desch and NCRC. He hadn't anticipated the relentless pressure when he'd returned to Dayton after his studies in Boston at MIT.

The machine clanked then stopped. Mark held his breath and prayed mechanical sounds would replace the sudden silence

"Again?" John Fields rubbed a handkerchief over his face and shoved it in his back pocket. "Maybe this problem is beyond us."

Grabbing his tools and moving toward the machine, Mark shrugged, refusing to admit defeat. "We'll tear it apart again. Find the trigger."

"Why waste our time? We're making the machine go too fast."

"You know the navy won't lower that requirement." Mark didn't blame the navy. Thousands of German messages were intercepted each day but would remain gibberish until they found a way to break through the scrambling the Enigma machines used to create a code. Without that breakthrough, the convoys sailing the Atlantic continued to be torpedoed by German U-boats. The war couldn't be won when all the men and materials crossing the Atlantic sank to the bottom. "We have to get this right."

"At least you're single. Alice isn't happy with the hours I'm keeping."

As Mark helped remove the front of the machine, he tried to ignore the sting from John's words. He didn't want to be single. He'd love nothing more than to settle down. But none of the girls he knew ever quite fit him. His current girl, Paige Winslow, came closest, but it had only been a few weeks. Too early to know what could develop between them, but he hoped. . .for what? Someone who would understand him? Someone to put up with the quirks of his job? Someone who supported him as he used his education in the war effort?

That shouldn't be too much to ask.

A sailor entered the room and motioned to Mark, who jolted to his feet. "Sorry, John. I've got to go."

John stared at him. "You're leaving? Just like that?"

"Um. . .yep. I promised to help transport the WAVES to quarters."

A knowing grin spread across John's face. "I see. Maybe I should join you."

"Mr. Happily Married? Don't think so." Mark slapped John on the shoulder. "See you tomorrow." He reached the door and nodded at the sailor. "Ready for me?"

"Yes, sir." The sailor turned and headed down the hallway, leaving Mark to hurry to follow.

Mark's mother had talked him into helping the WAVES. He'd be one of a handful of men surrounded by seventy women. It might appeal if he didn't have a steady girl. But what kind of woman joined the military? His Paige was the picture of femininity, much like his mother and his sister Josie. Now his kid sister Kat with her love for all things rough and tumble could join the WAVES. He shook his head at the thought. God help the WAVES if she decided to enlist.

Two buses waited outside Building 26. A handful of men loitered next to them. "Was I the last?"

"Yes, sir." The sailor grinned. "Guess you got distracted. If you'll climb aboard, we'll go." He checked his watch. "Their train arrives in ten minutes."

Mark climbed on the nearest bus and settled into the seat behind the driver. What could he do to help these women? Take their bags, stow them, and carry them to the right cabin?

The buses drove through the National Cash Register complex, then up Main Street. The station sat at Sixth and Ludlow, and Mark could hear the *whoosh* of a train's arrival as he climbed off the bus.

"This way." The same sailor led the way to the track.

If these gals traveled with half the luggage his sisters did, Mark would feel it tomorrow. What had he agreed to?

He leaned against the train station wall and watched. Soon a stream of women in navy suits disembarked. One led the way to the sailor. She seemed to have an extra insignia or two on her lapels.

"Are you ready for us, Ensign?"

The ensign snapped to attention. "Yes, ma'am."

"At ease, sailor."

"Yes, ma'am." He pointed back through the station. "The buses are out front."

"Thank you. We're eager to see our new quarters."

Mark worked his way through the gaggle of women to the baggage car. He reached for the nearest bag. A gloved hand touched his.

"I'll take that." He looked up into a composed, weary face. The gray eyes arrested his attention.

"Ma'am, I'm here to help with the bags."

"I'm sure that's kind of you, but I can handle mine."

From the set of her chin, it looked like she'd made up her mind, but this might be her first experience with Midwestern hospitality. Mark tightened his grip and smiled. "I'm sure you're capable, but I'm here to make certain your transition to your cabin goes smoothly. Please let me. I insist."

Her fingers loosened on the handle, but Mark wasn't sure it was because of his charm and welcoming words. He had a sneaking suspicion it was the word *cabin* that stopped her. Interesting. Almost as intriguing as the hint of tears in her eyes.

two

Evelyn felt singed by the heat in the man's gaze. He might claim his act was service in the guise of Midwestern hospitality, but it felt like a contest of wills. After a broken heart, she'd promised herself she'd never trust another man with anything important to her. But did she really want to carry that heavy suitcase another step?

Slowly, she released her grip and stepped back. "Thank you."

He continued to appraise her in a way that left heat climbing her cheeks, even as his look remained a far cry from the kind she usually received from men. Maybe her appearance didn't match his expectations. The man secured his grip on the bag, then tipped his head. "It's my pleasure. My name's Mark Miller. Welcome to Dayton."

"Thank you." She tipped her chin. "It will be an experience."

He chuckled and nodded. "That it will. The buses are through the station. Go ahead, I'll be right behind you with your bag."

She turned around and hid her hot cheeks. It didn't appear Mr. Miller intended to make fun of her, but he had no plans to back down on his. . .chivalry.

"What has you all bothered?" Viv's quiet voice pulled Evelyn from her churning thoughts.

"What do you make of that man?"

"The one carrying your bag?"

Evelyn nodded.

"He's handsome and volunteered to help. Relax and appreciate the assistance, Miss Independence."

The girl was right. It was nice to have someone attend to her needs. As Evelyn climbed on the first bus, she reminded herself not to get used to it. The WAVES wouldn't feel spoiled for long. "Guess I'll enjoy the help."

Evelyn turned in her seat and watched out the window as Mr. Miller deposited her case into the bowels of the bus. He made the large case look weightless.

"He is quite handsome," Viv teased.

She had to agree. The man moved with the grace of a weekend athlete.

Lonnie settled into the seat across the aisle from Viv and Evelyn. "Where do you think they'll billet us?"

"Definitely not on a boat." Viv answered.

Evelyn shook her head. "Isn't that a river over there? Maybe they've docked a boat along it for us."

The gals chuckled as the buses pulled out of the station. They drove by a Biltmore. Evelyn knew they wouldn't be lucky enough to stay at a hotel like that. But what could Mr. Miller mean by cabin? The image that flashed into her mind was filled with drafty rooms and mosquitoes. The drive wasn't long, and she tried to take in the feel of the small city. After a few minutes, the buses turned into a wooded acreage. Tall trees lined the property with its scattered buildings of all sizes.

"Welcome to Sugar Camp, ladies. Please follow me to your new home." Lt. Meyers ushered them into a large building that looked like a cafeteria. "Go to the front tables to get your cabin assignments."

Cabin? Evelyn's hope that Mr. Miller was misinformed crashed to the ground. "This is a change from basic training." Those dormitories had made her feel claustrophobic. Didn't sound like that would be much of a problem here.

Viv nodded. "You can say that again."

By the time Evelyn reached the front of the line and collected her cabin assignment, she was ready to collapse. Who'd have thought travel would take that much out of a gal? She plodded back to the bus, ready to collect her suitcase and satchel. Mr. Miller stood there, the sweat lining his forehead an indication he hadn't spent the last hour waiting for her.

"Carry your bag for you?" he asked, but the glint in his eyes let her know the expected answer. Frankly, she welcomed the help. She longed for a chance to recuperate from the travel, preferably in a nice, warm bubble bath. "Thank you, kind sir."

She gave him the number of the cabin, and he led the way across the camp. "You're over here."

The cabins looked small. Maybe there were only a couple of people per cabin. But if that was the case, there must be another dozen cabins hidden on the grounds. Mark knocked on the door and opened it. He placed the bag inside and stepped back out. "Here you go."

"This is home?" The thought had Evelyn ready to take her bag, hike right back to the train station, and go home to Washington DC. She hadn't expected the Biltmore, but this—it was ridiculous. The cabin smelled musty with a hint of mold that tickled her nose.

"Good luck." He turned to leave.

"Thank you." She closed the door behind him.

A chill filled the small room. Its walls were uncovered wood paneling. She supposed it held a rustic charm, but not exactly how she planned to live. It looked like original plans called for the room to hold two twin beds with side tables and lamps mounted into the wall. Between them stood a built-in closet. Probably adequate accommodations for two women, but someone had transformed each bed into bunks, suggesting four would live in the small space.

"Do they really expect four. . .here?" The thought of being stacked on top of other people made her stomach churn. She enjoyed people more than most, but this—

"You don't have to look so excited about sharing with me." Vivian poked her head around an inside door and stuck her tongue out. "Here's the bathroom. Looks like it leads to another bedroom." The small woman shivered. "This cabin could use some heat."

Evelyn gazed around the room but couldn't find a heater or radiator system. The blankets lining each bed looked impossibly thin. "Be glad we're here for the summer."

Viv nodded. "That's right. Though it doesn't feel like summer yet."

No, with the clouds ready to drop rain at the slightest provocation, a heavy dampness permeated the area. Evelyn could feel it to her bones.

The main door opened, and two more women entered the room.

"Hey, gals. I managed to change my cabin assignment and am with you after all." Merriment filled Lonnie's eyes as she dropped her bag. She pointed to the gal next to her. "This lovely lady is our new roommate Mary Ellen. Just met her in the cafeteria."

A woman with dark hair, glasses, and a pleasantly plump build, Mary Ellen walked over to one of the lower bunks, plopped her suitcase on top of it, and without a word began unpacking. Evelyn had to fight the urge to tell the woman to wait until they'd had an opportunity to decide who would live where.

Viv grinned at her. "Don't worry. I'll take a top bunk."

"Thanks." Evelyn watched the activity and had the unsettled feeling she'd been plopped in the middle of a hurricane. Silly girl, she hadn't thought hurricanes reached as far inland as Ohio.

ès

The next morning, Mark sat in the weekly meeting, rubbing his aching shoulders. He needed to spend more time on the baseball diamond if that little bit of lifting yesterday had him all tense.

"Time is running out." Admiral Meader's voice echoed through the cold, concrete room. He marched back and forth in front of the assembled engineers and machinists. "Each day that we don't have a working machine leads to more Allied deaths on the Atlantic."

Mark scrunched lower in his seat.

"What do they expect us to do?" John spoke behind his hand toward Mark.

"Work 'round the clock."

"I thought we were already doing that."

Meader walked toward them. "Do you gentlemen have anything to add?"

"No, sir," Mark mumbled.

"We're planning an invasion of the mainland, but German U-boat attacks still have our convoys reeling. We have to break these codes. Whatever it takes. If we work around the clock, so be it." He turned back to the rest of the room. "Any questions?"

There were none. The problem came in the lack of solutions.

No matter how many different ways Mark approached the problem, he couldn't see a way to make the machines cooperate.

The Germans had a machine they called Enigma. It scrambled the German messages into gibberish by spinning a message through four different wheels, each spin changing the letter combinations. The British, with the help of Polish scientists, had broken the code when the machine contained three interchangeable wheels. Then the Germans added a fourth wheel, and the code became unbreakable. The United States landed the challenge of breaking the four-wheel code. The Bombes were designed to race through calculations, but so far, the machines only excelled at breaking down or springing oil leaks, not solving codes.

Something had to be done, but no matter where they turned, the problem loomed bigger than any solution.

That wasn't good enough.

Every day, that message was pounded into their heads. Even if Meader and the other navy bigwigs didn't remind them, the newspaper headlines were sufficient.

Some days, Mark wished he'd never accepted the position.

The meeting finally ended, and Mark and John returned to their Bombe.

John eyed the machine. "Adam looks tired."

"Just your imagination."

"Maybe we should give him the day off."

Mark snorted and watched the techs work on the machine. A quick visual inspection indicated the seals had held overnight.

The Enigma machine was small, barely filling a hard-sided valise. In contrast, the Bombe stood a foot taller than Mark and wider than a good-sized davenport. That meant a lot of computing power trying to break a code with possible combinations that ranged in the millions. Astronomical numbers.

The door opened, and Mark looked up. Who could be coming in? He knew everybody who had access.

His jaw almost dropped when he spotted a group of gals dressed in WAVES uniforms.

One of the gals looked around, then took a step back. "I'm sorry. I don't think we're supposed to be here."

John stepped between the women and Adam. "You're right. Only those with clearance are allowed."

An MP, one of the military police stationed in Building 26, hurried in the room, a sheepish expression on his face. "Ladies, you'll need to leave."

Mark watched. Someone would have to learn why no one guarded the door. This was exactly the kind of breach that they guarded against. What were these dames supposed to do other than get in the way and distract the single guys from their jobs? This couldn't be a good idea. No, with the pressure the navy had on them to find a solution yesterday, any distractions here in Building 26 were a bad idea.

❧

Evelyn followed the other WAVES into the large room. She hadn't expected the silence. She had assumed the hum of the machine would fill the room with a low roar. Then she noticed the men scrambling around the machine, though a couple stared at the WAVES like they'd intruded on sacred ground. This machine looked like a marvel of modern engineering. The magnitude of wiring and components welded and soldered together impressed her.

"What do you make of that?" Vivian gestured to the machine.

"I'm not sure." Evelyn edged closer. She'd never seen anything like it. "They've strung processors together." She longed to analyze the machine. They must be working on something amazingly complex to need such power. Code breaking?

"Ladies, I'm sorry, but we've made a mistake." Lt. Meyers hurried in from the hall. "Please follow me."

"Won't some of us help with these machines?" Evelyn hoped so.

"No, Ensign Happ. Not at this time." Lt. Meyers urged them toward the door. "If you'll follow me, it's time for the rest of your orientation."

The other WAVES turned to file out, but Evelyn stood rooted to the floor. She wanted to understand every element of how the machine was constructed and what it could do. She'd studied all those years for an opportunity like this. Excitement pulsed through her.

This was why she'd joined the WAVES.

"Are you joining us, Ensign Happ?" Lt. Meyers cleared her throat.

Evelyn jerked out of her reverie and found one of the men openly watching her. Mark? Yes, the man who'd helped her yesterday. So he was part of this endeavor. That would explain his presence at the train station, though he didn't look like a valet today. His eyes were guarded. What had happened to all that Midwestern hospitality? She noted his broad shoulders and the dark hair that waved around his forehead and ears. Not the typical engineer build. When he didn't break eye contact, she winked at him, then turned on her heel. "Lead on."

&

That night, Evelyn crossed the wooded compound of Sugar Camp from her cabin to the chapel. She followed a steady flow of women filing into the building. Seventy voices quieted at Admiral Meader's command, and the WAVES sat forward on the pews. Evelyn thought they all looked eager to learn more about why they'd come to Dayton. As far as she was concerned, the machines were enough reason, but the other WAVES weren't likely to appreciate them.

Admiral Meader moved to the front of the room, behind a table. A small man with an intense, brooding look sat at the table. Lt. Meyers sat next to him, back ramrod straight, uniform perfect in every detail.

The admiral surveyed the women. "Ladies, you are here to assist with a top-secret military project. You will play a critical role in building parts for the machines, maintaining the machines, and eventually running them.

"But you may never talk to anyone about the job you do in Building 26. Not even among yourselves. If any of you talk, you will immediately be removed to St. Elizabeth's Hospital, where you will serve the rest of the war."

St. Elizabeth's? Where was that? Not that Evelyn was interested in finding out. Everyone treated this project gravely, signifying its importance. "The success of this project is critical to the overall war effort. Accordingly, you must treat it carefully and make sure your lips never become loose about the work you do here.

"If you feel you are unable to do that, tell us now, and we'll remove you from the location immediately."

Vivian leaned closer to Evelyn. "Is he serious?"

Evelyn studied the commander's intent stare and the serious lines around his eyes and mouth. "Yes, I think so."

three

"Join us for the night off?" John invited Mark to join a group of engineers and WAVES headed out for a good time. Only a week since the arrival of the WAVES, and already the atmosphere in Building 26 had changed. Mark had known it would happen.

The WAVES might not work in the rooms with the Bombes, but their presence was felt throughout the building. From the rooms where they soldered components to the cafeteria where they spent breaks and meals, the women had men forgetting who they were and why they were in Dayton.

The men were more than willing to give up the routine and mind-numbing chores to the WAVES. Mark had heard more than one man admit he was glad he didn't have to solder any more gadgets and gizmos for the machines.

As soon as Desch told everyone to go home after hitting another wall with the Bombes, several of the guys had hurried off to find WAVES equally ready to hit the town. Now John and his wife planned to join the mix.

The handful of WAVES looked excited, and the men appeared just as eager to show them around. Mark eyed the group, looking for the brunette he'd helped earlier. He hadn't seen her since the detour the day after the WAVES arrived. She had an intelligence and curiosity in her gaze and had lingered so long that he wondered if she understood the machine's purpose. If she were part of the group, maybe he'd join them. What was he thinking? He should spend the time with Paige.

"Not tonight, folks. Have a good time." He'd call Paige. See if she could join him for dinner.

Mark called her from a pay phone on the first floor. He

tapped the glass of the booth as he waited for Paige to pick up. It had been too long since they'd had time together during the week. He'd take her to a restaurant, maybe to a movie. After a dozen rings, he hung up. His shoulders slumped, and the evening felt empty. Maybe he could catch the others after all. He hurried from the booth, but couldn't find them. Guess he'd go home early tonight. Not the ideal way to spend a rare night off.

As Mark trudged the blocks home from NCR, he felt the nip in the air. He wouldn't mind sunshine breaking through, but it didn't look like it would happen.

Desch had hinted they might get the weekend off if they made a breakthrough tomorrow on the machines. Maybe Mark would get to play a game of baseball with some guys. Kat, his kid sister, would probably tag along, but she'd done that since she was five. She'd been cute then. Now she bordered on a woman who made the men stop and stare. He wasn't sure how he felt about that. Having Josie married off to a good man was one thing. But he couldn't imagine Kat paired off. Fortunately, she lingered on the border of a kid. Sixteen, almost seventeen. Way too young for anything serious.

Yeah, that's what he'd keep telling himself.

He turned up the sidewalk on Volusia Avenue, stately trees shading the avenue and lending substance to the area. A minute later, he stood on his parents' front porch.

The front door opened, and Kat barreled toward him.

"It's about time you got here."

"What?" He staggered back a step as she tackled him.

"I've got news. Big news. The kind of news that will amaze you."

"Really?" Kat lived life at high speed. Mark couldn't imagine what had her so excited this time. "Do I get a sneak peek at the news?"

She shook her head as she pulled him up the steps. "No, you have to wait to hear with Dad. So come on. We're sitting down to eat."

Mark chuckled as she led him down the hallway.

"Mom, I'll wash my hands and be right in."

Kat stuck her tongue out at him and hurried into the dining room. Mark could hear her voice filtering through the door as he washed up. Something had her over the moon.

He strode into the dining room and stopped at his mom's side long enough to kiss her on the cheek. "Evening, Mother, Dad."

He settled into his chair and unfolded the napkin onto his lap.

"Now that you're here, maybe we can hear Kat's news." Dad smiled at his baby girl. "What's going on?"

"I got an invitation to tryouts for the All-American Girls Professional Softball League."

Mark choked on his water and quickly set the glass down. "The what?"

"If you weren't so wrapped up in your job, you'd know. Mr. Wrigley is starting a league. Tryouts are open to anyone, but it's better if you get an invitation. I did. Today. In the mail." She shrieked.

"Congratulations, Kat." Mom took another bite of roast, then asked, "Do you want to accept?"

Kat stared at her, fork in midair. "Of course."

Mom and Dad exchanged a glance. Mark rolled his eyes. This conversation would be very short. By morning, Kat would have permission and pack her bags.

"Girls playing softball? Professionally?" Mark couldn't resist tweaking her nose.

"I've only played since I was six." Kat crossed her arms. "Remember? You took me with you. Taught me to play with all your friends. Kept making me play."

The table erupted in laughter. "Yeah, that's what I did. Forced you to play." He reached across the table and ruffled her curls. "Congrats, kid. If that's what you want, go play with a bunch of girls. It'll be boring compared to playing with me and my friends."

"Yeah. But none of you offered to pay me more than fifty dollars a week to play."

She had a point there.

❧

Evelyn walked across Sugar Camp from the dining hall to her cabin. As she walked, she passed the recreation center, theater, and baseball diamond. Maybe when it warmed up, she'd spend some time at the pool. Anything would be better than the march to Building 26, followed by a long day soldering rotors, the march home, and a meal. The routine was only a couple of days old but already drove her crazy.

There had to be more.

Many of the WAVES had hunkered down in their rooms to avoid the nippy night.

She stopped as she neared the chapel. She'd never spent much time in church. Her family had kept Sundays for sleeping in and the occasional game of golf. In college, she joined a roommate at a small church in downtown Lafayette several times. Peace had always engulfed her there, but she'd leave and rush right back into the cycle of classes and homework. Basic training had been equally busy. Now her life had emptied of busyness—at least of the sort she'd known at home and school.

No, the navy would keep her occupied, but it wasn't a cerebral exercise. Not yet.

Evelyn stopped at the steps to the chapel, hand on the railing. Should she go in? But what would she do? Sit in the cold chapel? Or return to the cabin and curl up on her bed with the blanket wrapped around her shoulders? Neither sounded overly appealing, but she knew what would happen if she went back to her cabin. Nothing beyond reading a book.

She hesitated on the first step, then turned and headed to her cabin. Her shoulders slumped as she trudged to her room. She felt the weight of. . .something. She didn't know what to call it. A presence? All she knew was she felt empty and exposed. Somehow lacking.

She looked over her shoulder, expecting to find someone watching her. She didn't like the sensation. Evelyn tried to shake it. On the next free night, she'd lead the charge for an evening out with her dancing shoes, even if she had to wear her navy WAVES uniform. Anything to avoid the inner searching that plagued her tonight.

❧

The next morning, Evelyn hurried through the race to dress. Eight women using one bathroom presented more than its share of challenges. She needed to purchase her own mirror. With four women squeezed in front of the mirror in the mornings, her odds of getting ready without an elbow to the face were horribly slim.

After a near miss with her cheek, she tossed her lipstick down and backed out of the bathroom. "Let me know when it's safe to return."

Giggles flowed from the gals.

"Come on, Evelyn." Viv stepped around the door. "Don't get sore. We're all doing what we have to."

"No problem. Just trying to avoid looking like a clown at work. Too many elbows and bodies crammed in one spot."

"I'll say." Lonnie bounced into the room, every hair perfectly in place and her lipstick expertly applied. "Welcome to life with oodles of women."

Mary Ellen scurried in. "The room's free now."

"Thanks." Evelyn walked into the bathroom and laughed. Her lipstick had disappeared in a sea of toiletries. "Anyone mind if I use their things?"

Three women filled the doorway, giggling.

"Guess we'll get to know each other really well." Evelyn smiled and grabbed a random tube. If she didn't hurry, she'd miss breakfast at Building 26.

An hour later after a quick breakfast in the cafeteria with the rest of the gals, she strode down the hall toward her assigned room. The urge to enter the room with the Bombe pulled at her. She should keep walking. Do as she was told. But when she reached the door, no MPs were present to keep her out. What could it hurt to peek? The engineer in her wanted to see the machine. The woman in her wanted to know if Mark Miller was around. Something about him intrigued her in a way that made her ignore the rules. What did she have to lose anyway? No one was around to stop her. She opened the door and entered, her heels snapping against the concrete floor. Men halted mid-motion. She tried to ignore them as she looked for Mark and then at the machine. Based on the oil pooled at the Bombe's base, it must have sprung a leak overnight.

"Does it do that often?"

"What?" The man she'd broken the rules for stared at her.

"Leak oil." She pointed at the spill.

Mark's mouth pulled down in a tight frown. He studied her a moment. "How did you get in here?"

"Walked in."

He looked her up and down, his frown deepening. "That doesn't mean you can come in. You aren't on the list. The one at the door that someone is supposed to check."

Evelyn struggled to find a response, but her throat tightened until she felt strangled. It wasn't often a man made her even a bit tongue-tied. "Why can't I help? I have the training and background."

"It doesn't matter. Unless you're on that list, you can't be here." He stepped toward her, blocking her ability to step farther into the room. "We're here to troubleshoot. Try to engineer ahead of the problems. That requires access to information, and if you haven't noticed, information is tightly controlled around here."

She raised an eyebrow. The answer seemed too simplistic. All right. She could understand that at one level. The navy made its rules and lived by them without question. So she needed to give him a reason to work with her and push her case to the higher-ups. "How often do these leaks happen?"

Wariness swept over the man. "What? Did I say something wrong?"

"We aren't allowed to talk about the machines. Especially with unauthorized personnel." Mark's quiet words carried a punch. "Aren't you supposed to be soldering rotors?"

She didn't want to acknowledge his words, not when she could do so much more. "What if they assigned me to work here?"

Mark studied her closely. "How do you think that would happen? The WAVES brought you here and gave you a position. Seems that's the end of the matter."

"Really?" Evelyn crossed her arms and stared at him. "Does it help to know I have an engineering degree from Purdue University?"

"I'm sure that's great, but that's a small school. Most of us come from MIT. Ever heard of it?" He grabbed her elbow and marched her away from the machine and toward the door.

Maybe mystery wasn't so attractive after all. And maybe he wouldn't take her any more seriously than others had. She squared her shoulders and stared up at him. Even with her pumps, she was dwarfed by him. "I think you may be as shortsighted as most of the men out there. I worked just as hard for my engineering degree as any of you, may have received better grades. And if you think I can't contribute to solving your engineering problems, well, I hope it doesn't delay the success of this project." She bit the inside of her mouth to stop the stream of words and to distract from the stinging behind her eyes. "If you'll excuse me."

Evelyn pulled from his grip and exited the room. She tried to keep her steps steady and slow. It was only when she put distance between the room and her that she allowed herself to run down the wide hallway to the women's restroom.

She shouldn't have believed she could do something special as a WAVES. It appeared these men weren't any more ready to see a woman contribute than the others she'd encountered.

She sniffled and fought to pull herself together as she stared in the bathroom mirror. She would not let anyone see how deeply that cut. Somehow she'd find a way to be trusted with this vital project.

four

Saturday, Mark couldn't shake the feeling that he'd treated Evelyn poorly. Even as he went through the steps of playing a game of baseball—something that usually brought him pleasure—he thought he'd been too harsh.

He'd seen the tears she'd tried so hard to conceal. Maybe having sisters made him soft, but he hated that his words had caused her pain. It wasn't her fault they didn't know her clearance yet. And if she really did have a degree from a school like Purdue, she might bring a fresh perspective to the challenges with the Bombes. Some of the men didn't like having any women around, thought the WAVES in their uniforms were only there to torment and distract them. But what if Evelyn could do more than the task assigned? What if she could see the problem differently? Bring a fresh approach to the problem?

Did Desch and Admiral Meader have any idea of her background? He should mention it. Make sure they knew.

A ball hit him in the chest, and he groaned.

"You okay, baby?" Paige's voice carried from the bleachers.

"Yeah, Mark, you hurt?" Kat grinned at him from her shortstop position. "You really should get your head in the game or get out."

He had to give it to her. He'd certainly used that line on her a time or two. "Maybe I'll sit out the next inning."

"Good idea." Kat turned back toward home plate, all business.

When the inning ended, Mark scanned the crowd for Paige. She waved at him from her spot, and he jogged to her.

"That looked like it hurt." She ran her fingers along his face, as if searching it for injuries.

30

Deciding he enjoyed her caress too much, he stepped to the side. "I'm fine. I think I'll watch the rest of the game next to you."

A smile brightened her face, and she slipped her arm through his, anchoring him to her side. "I'd like that. I wish you had more weekends like this."

Mark wanted to explain why his job required so much, but that wasn't an option. She had to live in the dark along with everyone else. "Let's enjoy this one."

The petite woman snuggled next to his side, and Mark wrapped his arm around her shoulders. Paige might be at an outdoor ballgame, but she'd dressed for an afternoon tea. Her short-sleeved dress and fancy hat looked out of place among the crowd. Why would this fashion plate choose to spend her time with him? Paige could have about any man. He didn't know the answer to this question, but he pulled her closer and vowed to enjoy every moment they had together.

She looked up at him, eyebrows raised. "Yes?"

"Merely enjoying your presence, mademoiselle."

A knowing grin softened her face and lit her hazel eyes. "See that you do, sir."

The inning ended, and Mark savored every moment of the sun's rays on his face. It was entirely too rare of a sensation. The wartime schedule might be fifty-four hours a week, but the demands of his job often pushed the workweek closer to eighty hours. Far too much time spent inside. Days like this outside the four walls of some manmade structure were what he needed.

The team played better as he sat next to Paige. Why wouldn't it? It wasn't like he made it to practice. Even this early in the season, he'd been pretty much AWOL.

"Let's get out of here." Paige's voice purred in his ear. When she talked like that, it was hard to tell her no.

"What do you have in mind?"

"Let's walk across the park and go to the theater. Maybe grab some dinner."

Sounded expensive, but he lived at home with minimal costs. Who was he kidding? A beautiful lady wanted to spend her Saturday with him. "Let's run by my house first, and I'll clean up. Then let's see what we find."

After a quick change at home, Mark borrowed his father's car. They headed back downtown and grabbed a bite at a local café before strolling the streets. He tried to focus on Paige's commentary, but his thoughts betrayed him by returning to Adam.

"You're distracted." Her lips pouted.

Mark looked at her hand where it rested on his arm. "It's been a long week."

"But you're with me now. Can't you forget everything else for a while? I don't get to see enough of you."

"I'm sorry. I've tried." How he'd tried. They ambled the block in silence. "What do you see in me?" They stopped walking, and he looked into her eyes, curious to know her thoughts. "I'm an engineer with no plans to leave Dayton. I work a job that demands long hours from me. I practically neglect you because of it. Are you with me only because I'm not in uniform and haven't left to fight the war?"

"There is that." Her smile died under his stare. "For goodness' sakes, Mark, I'm kidding." She turned from him and continued down the sidewalk. "You're a man who's sure of himself and his God. Yes, you're busy and I rarely get to see you, but when I do, you ask crazy questions like this. There's little surface banter." She looked up at him and sighed. "Sometimes I wish there was more of that, but I'll take what you have to offer."

Mark followed her and wondered why her answer wasn't good enough. It felt like she'd pulled out a yardstick and he measured in the "nice but not lovable" category.

He didn't want to be someone's time-filler while they waited for something better to come along. Paige was more than that to him. Beauty infused her from the inside out, she lived patience and virtue teaching children all week, and she chose to spend time with him because she liked him.

What more could he possibly want from a woman?

❧

Saturday afternoon, Evelyn joined a group of women headed to a tea at Mr. Desch's home. The constant dressing like the other WAVES left her feeling unoriginal, so she'd decided to stake her claim on individuality. She pinned a broach on her jacket.

When Viv saw it, she laughed. "Is that the best you can do? A flower broach?"

"One has to work with what one owns."

"Then we need to shop. If you're going to poke at the rules, at least do it with some style that doesn't say 'this is my grandmother's.'"

"How about colored gloves?" Lonnie tossed a pair at her.

"In the summer?"

"You'd definitely be the only one wearing them."

Mary Ellen looked her over. "I think you need an anchor broach. At least that alludes to the navy."

Evelyn shook her head. "The idea is to tweak this incredibly boring uniform. Add some personality to it. How can one go to a tea looking exactly like everyone else?"

"It simply isn't done." Viv shook her head.

"Exactly." Evelyn caught the glint in Viv's eye and took a step toward her. "Are you poking fun at me?"

"Me?" Viv slipped back. "Never."

"If we don't plan to walk, we need to leave." Mary Ellen stood at the door, chewing on a fingernail.

The ribbing continued until the bus arrived at the Desches' small home. Evelyn didn't mind, especially as others joined in. Maybe they would add their own little statements of individuality. It would certainly make things more interesting.

As soon as they stepped in the backyard, Evelyn could tell Mrs. Desch liked to entertain. A group of women stood next to their hostess near tables loaded with finger foods and drinks. They seemed determined to welcome the WAVES with style.

Mrs. Desch looked as if she'd walked off the pages of *Vogue* magazine.

Evelyn couldn't wait to meet the intense man's wife. "I wonder if she's anything like him."

Lonnie strolled next to her, her purse laced across her chest. "I doubt it. Opposites attract."

Mrs. Desch stepped toward them. "Welcome, ladies. We're so glad you could join us. I hope you will enjoy this break from your labors and the opportunity to relax with new friends. There's no agenda other than getting to know each other."

Evelyn looked at her roommates. "Guess that's our signal."

Viv nodded. "Time to mingle and make nice."

Lonnie took off for a table loaded with cookies and other sweets. Mary Ellen trailed behind her.

A smartly dressed older woman approached Evelyn. "Hello, I'm Marjorie Miller."

"Evelyn Happ."

"That's a beautiful name." The woman gestured toward a set of chairs, interest in her eyes. "Would you like to join me?"

"Thank you."

"First, let's get something to drink." The stately woman walked to the beverages. She filled glasses with iced tea for both of them and offered one to Evelyn. Mrs. Miller led the way to the chairs, tugging off her gloves as she settled into her seat. She took a sip of her tea and leaned forward with a smile. "I enjoy meeting new people but always find the first minutes unsettling. It's almost like those first dances one attends as a student. Who will interest me and find me interesting?"

Evelyn laughed. "That description is pretty apt." She looked around the yard. The other women had clustered in small groups. "I'm still finding my way around town."

Marjorie eyed her over her glass of tea. "Then I think I'll adopt you. You need someone to show you around, and you can escape to our home when you need a break from wherever the navy has you stashed."

The offer sounded wonderful. "Thank you, Mrs. Miller."

"Start by calling me Marjorie. Mrs. Miller is my husband's mother. Now tell me about yourself. You're at Sugar Camp, aren't you?"

How did the woman know?

"Don't worry, dear. It's impossible to miss you gals when they close the road and you march to work. That is quite a sight."

In no time, Mrs. Miller had pulled many details from Evelyn and made her feel like she'd known the woman for years. "My son, Mark, works in Building 26 with Mrs. Desch's husband."

"We've met a few times."

The fashionable woman quirked an eyebrow at her.

"He's been quite helpful, though he's protective of his project."

"That's my Mark." Pride bloomed across Mrs. Miller's face. "How do you like your work?"

Evelyn tried to think of a diplomatic way to answer. "It's important."

Mrs. Miller studied her. "But not what you expected?"

"Not really."

The woman patted her hand. "Sometimes God uses the trying times to teach us important lessons."

"Doesn't that require one to actually believe?"

"No. Sometime the lesson is what attracts us to Him. I've found Him to be a gentle yet persistent wooer." Mrs. Miller smiled, a gentle peace radiating from her countenance. "If you seek Him, He just might surprise you."

Evelyn started to politely, yet firmly decline, when something stopped her. "Maybe I will."

"I'd like to have you join my family for lunch tomorrow. Come to church, too, if you like, or we could pick you up after service. We don't live far from Sugar Camp. Promise you'll join us."

"Yes, ma'am." The cafeteria at Sugar Camp might be open twenty-four hours a day, but its fare couldn't be as good as a home-cooked meal. She'd be a fool not to accept the offer.

Before Evelyn quite knew what had happened, she had agreed to a time for the Millers to pick her up for morning services. Marjorie excused herself to meet some other members of the WAVES. She patted Evelyn's hand as she stood up. "It was so nice to meet you, Evelyn. I look forward to seeing you again tomorrow."

Vivian settled into the chair Mrs. Miller had vacated. "You look a bit stunned."

"You could say that." Evelyn leaned back and absorbed the new dynamic. "Looks like I've been adopted by Mrs. Miller."

"That's nice."

"Umm." Evelyn didn't know which she dreaded more: conversations about a God she didn't know anything about, or more time with a man who didn't see her as anything more than another empty-headed woman.

❧

Sunday morning, Evelyn waited at the entrance to Sugar Camp for the Millers to pick her up. Constantly being in uniform certainly had one advantage: she didn't have to waste time deciding what to wear. Several of her cabin mates had also made plans to attend services but had scattered to churches around Dayton. Soon, a Studebaker pulled next to her, and Mrs. Miller waved her over.

"I'm so glad you joined us." Mrs. Miller introduced Evelyn to her husband Louis and daughter Kat. "Climb in back with Kat."

In no time, the small group hurried up the steps of the Christ Community Church. Anxious thoughts ran through Evelyn's mind. What if she didn't like the services? How could she leave? And what if she didn't like the church? Would she regret depending on others for transportation? Too late to worry now. She set her shoulders and pasted a bright smile on her face as she followed the Millers into the fellowship hall.

Mrs. Miller clasped Evelyn's hands. "My husband will go ahead and grab a pew for us. I'd like to introduce you to some friends."

Evelyn followed Marjorie into the sanctuary, pausing as the woman made sure she met everyone they passed. Mr. Miller had held their seats for ten minutes before they made their way to the front. Kat had stopped to chat with other girls, a quiet but animated discussion.

Someone touched Evelyn's shoulder, and she turned to find Mark Miller standing in the aisle.

"Is there room for me in this pew? The others are filling up."

Evelyn turned and surveyed the room. He was right. She eased closer to Marjorie.

Mark leaned over Evelyn to talk to his mom. "You didn't tell me Evelyn was your guest."

"I forgot to mention it." A twinkle graced Mrs. Miller's eyes. "But if I'd known—"

"I would have done it anyway." Her son sang the words with her.

While she waited for the service to begin, Evelyn examined the stained-glass windows. The images of a man praying desperately in a garden followed by a scene on a cross and the empty tomb intrigued her, but she didn't know what to make of them. No matter how many times she joined a friend at church, the story never made sense to her. Why would a relatively young man in His early thirties allow His life to be taken? Especially if He was truly the Son of God? But as Evelyn listened to the congregation sing and the pastor preach, she longed to understand.

Mark shifted against the hard pew. As he did, his shoulder brushed hers. The warmth of that small connection caused Evelyn to consider leaning closer and prolonging the connection rather than rushing to break it like she should.

What was it about this man that tied her stomach in knots and left her unsure? This one, he was different than others she knew—and in a way that appealed. She eased a breath of space between them and tuned back into the sermon.

It didn't take long to determine she had daydreamed through too much of it. The sermon made little sense catching bits and pieces. She looked around the sanctuary, her gaze resting on Mark.

He turned and caught her watching him. A knowing smile stretched across his mouth.

Part of her faltered at the way he could read her thoughts.

No one did that. But wasn't that what God wanted to do? Wasn't that why she'd steered clear of church? She didn't want to acknowledge God because that meant He knew everything about her. There could be no secrets or hidden spaces of her heart.

Mark turned his attention back to the front of the sanctuary, and she wondered what it would be like to live life known to the deepest parts of her soul.

five

May had almost evaporated, taking Kat with it. Mark hadn't stopped to think how quiet the house would be without his sister stomping around. Somehow, she'd talked her way onto a traveling team, while his life continued in its rut: work, try a new solution, watch that solution fail, work some more.

Some days he felt like an old man way before his time.

He should be grateful, he supposed. At least he was using his education in a way that served the war effort without picking up a rifle. Maybe he'd be more effective with a rifle. Debatable. He'd never hit anything smaller than the side of a shed.

Yep, call him the king of effectiveness.

By Monday, May 31, Mark was ready for something to happen. Adam had to start working, or the project could be over. They'd exhausted all the possibilities and configurations. Today, they'd test the machines yet again, and Mark prayed for a miracle.

Refreshed from the weekend, Mark entered Building 26, eager to take another crack at Adam. A machine was predictable. Rational. When it didn't work correctly, there should be a logical reason. The challenge lay in identifying the breakdown and rectifying it. He brushed by several marines as he made his way to Adam's room. About time they had sufficient men stationed to keep wanderers out. Maybe Evelyn's visits had reinforced the need for a constant presence. After the marine posted at the door checked his name against those listed on it, the guard allowed Mark to enter Adam's classroom.

John and several others stood around the room. It already felt closed in and stuffy. What he wouldn't give for windows.

Mark tossed his hat on the coat rack and hung his jacket.

"How'd the test runs go last night?"

John shrugged. "We haven't been debriefed yet. Ready to feed another message through this big boy?"

"Ready as I'll ever be." Much as Mark wanted this to work, he struggled to hold on to the hope that this time would be any different than the thousand other times the Bombe had wrestled with coded gibberish.

"All right." John waved at one of the technicians, who set the wheels to the assigned starting position.

Adam whirled to life. The noise soon reached a deafening pitch as the rotors and gears raced through an almost infinite number of cycles, trying to identify the one that would match that used by the Germans.

By having four wheels with twenty-six settings, the Germans had exponentially expanded the potential code settings. Up to 456,976 initial settings times 456,976 tumbler settings meant the Enigmas had an almost infinite number of configurations. The odds boggled Mark's mind. That impossible problem dominated his work each day. Mark glanced at his watch and saw the machine had already been at it for thirty minutes. This could take hours, if it ever did match the code. Maybe he should get coffee; let John and the others babysit the machine.

"Need anything from the cafeteria?"

John roused himself enough to shake his head. "Nah. I'll grab something when you get back." He looked the machine over. "So far no hitches."

Mark nodded. "But that doesn't mean this time we'll get the breakthrough."

"Oh ye of little faith."

True. But the constant failure had worn him down. Maybe they'd beat their heads against the wall until the end of the war. Never quite reach a breakthrough.

Boy, he'd developed a defeatist attitude. He needed to shake it off and move on. Mark marched to the door. Adam stopped, and Mark stilled. Could this be the time?

Silence almost as deafening as the noise had been minutes

before settled over the room. Mark considered banging his head against the door. Another short. They'd have to hunt it down and replace that part. All in an effort to get the machine up and running so it could break down again.

Then Adam backed up and stopped again. Mark and John stared at the machine, then at each other. Silence again filled the room. But a beautiful silence. The kind that meant the Bombe had a match.

They raced to Adam and pulled the printed story with its wheel positions from the machine's side.

Mark stared at the piece of paper. He took the piece to the mocked-up Enigma machine, set the Enigma to the corresponding settings, and entered the coded message. Gibberish printed out the other side. It looked like German, but someone fluent in the language would verify.

Hope pounded through Mark as he looked at the page. Maybe, just maybe, Adam had made a breakthrough.

ஒ

Evelyn sat at the table, trying to solder the intricate designs on the rotor in front of her. All those hours of fine needlework her mother had foisted on her paid off in the delicate and exacting work. These rotors must be part of the large machines in the guarded rooms.

The work put her mind to sleep, making it hard to stay focused.

Instead, she allowed her thoughts to wander over the people she'd met since arriving. Sunday at the Millers' had been. . .nice. Marjorie served as the perfect hostess, and Evelyn had felt welcome and included. Mark had disappeared soon after dinner when his girl called. Evelyn wondered why this woman hadn't joined them for church and Sunday dinner. The thought felt small. It wasn't her place to be jealous. What did it matter to her if Mark had a girl? It wasn't like she wanted the position.

Did she?

Of course not. She hadn't joined the WAVES to find a

man. But if she had, Mark Miller fit the bill. Smart. Good-looking. Kind.

Evelyn shook her head. She needed to focus on gaining experience, the kind that would help her turn her textbook knowledge into practical skills she could use. That was the least she could do to make this time in Dayton valuable.

Dayton certainly wasn't what she'd had in mind when she joined up and left her home in DC.

She'd thought to move from one city to another, but Dayton barely qualified with its 211,000 souls. The District had an urbane flair. Wartime energy pulsed through it. The parts of Dayton Evelyn had seen couldn't compare. And Mrs. Miller's home couldn't compare to her parents' place in Georgetown. During the Millers' Sunday dinners, ambassadors and congressmen didn't surround the table. Maybe that's why the conversation flowed and left Evelyn with a longing to return.

"All right, ladies. We'll take our break now." Charlotte Johnson, the room's den mom, took out her book while the other WAVES relaxed. In a soothing voice, she picked up reading *Little Women* where she had left off at the last break. Her voice had a peaceful quality that lulled many in the room to a restful state. Evelyn couldn't decide whether she liked it or it annoyed her. With each chapter, however, she found herself pulled deeper into the familiar tale. The only problem came when she envisioned Katharine Hepburn as Jo. Before the movie's release several years ago, she'd pictured Jo differently. Now Katharine's face intruded on her imagination.

Evelyn slipped out of her chair to walk to the restroom, her heels clicking loudly against the floor. Sunlight streamed through the windows, warming the walkway that vibrated with excitement. The marines stood at their posts, but others hurried up the hallway toward Adam's room. She followed a few steps behind, wondering if she could slip in and learn the source of excitement.

The marine at the door stopped her. "Your name."

"Evelyn Happ."

He looked at the list but didn't find her name. "I can't let you in."

"Please?" She batted her eyelashes and hoped he'd make an exception for her.

He stared at her and moved to block the door. "You aren't authorized."

"Sometimes I wish you all weren't so obstinate."

He looked past her, jaw sharply chiseled as granite.

"Fine." She brushed past him, fighting the urge to stamp her foot in frustration. Something had happened, and she'd probably never learn what. Especially when everyone lived under a vow of silence. She couldn't even talk to the women in her room about what they did. It would take someone with a head full of bricks to not realize the twenty-six points on the rotor corresponded to the twenty-six letters in the alphabet. All she wanted, no, *needed*, was to discuss the project with somebody who understood it.

This was an historic project. It had to be. The computing power in Adam was immense.

⁂

Mark and John whooped.

"I can't believe it." Mark ran his hand through his hair as he studied the machine. "Adam found something."

"How can we make sure this isn't a new malfunction?" Wary hope shone on John's face.

"Let's take the message and run it through Eve. If Adam made a hit, so will Eve."

John hurried to Adam and took the original message as well as the stop. He turned to the technicians. "Don't do anything with Adam until we return."

Mark and John hustled into the hallway and followed its labyrinthine path. They turned a corner, and Mark bounced into somebody.

A soft sound came from the woman as she landed on the floor.

"Excuse me." Mark reached down to help her up, as John tap-danced beside him.

"Come on, Mark. We've got to get to that room."

"Go ahead. I'll be right behind you."

The gal looked up at him, and he found himself staring into familiar gray eyes.

"Mr. Miller. Do you run into girls often?" Mischief was written across Evelyn Happ's face.

"Only on Mondays." He helped her to her feet.

"My lucky day. Where're you off to in such a hurry?"

He wanted to tell her. She might actually appreciate what they'd accomplished. When she looked at him with such expectation, he wished he could answer. But he couldn't. Answer once, and he could find himself on the Pacific front faster than he could say GI.

"Sorry." He shrugged. "You know the rules."

Her face fell, renewing the temptation to share his news. "Hopefully, the powers that be will let us know eventually."

"Maybe. I'd better catch John."

She nodded, but he found himself reluctant to let go of her hand and break the connection. "Will you join my family for church again this week?"

She paused as if to consider her words. "I think I'd like that. Your mother has been very kind to me."

"She's that sort. She likes to take people under her wing. Show them around. Right now, you're her protégée." He gave her a mock salute. "See you Sunday."

"Yes."

He felt her gaze as he rounded the corner and headed into Eve's room. Tension-filled engineers watched Eve as if their lives depended on her response to the code. Even Desch and Meader had come. Meader stood at ease, while Desch hunched in a chair. The stress and strain of the last months had marked the man bearing the brunt of the navy's pressure.

Mark prayed and paced the floor while Eve gyrated through configuration after configuration. Time crawled, and he wondered if they'd missed something with Adam's stop and reversal. Maybe Adam had simply malfunctioned, and they'd failed to recognize the signs of another breakdown. One they'd missed because they hadn't seen it yet. He crossed his arms and leaned against the wall. *Father, please let Eve find it, too.* They all needed the hope some success would bring. Thomas Edison might have said he found ten thousand ways not to make a light bulb before having success, but they didn't have the luxury of time for that many errors.

Men died every day. Others, too. He thought of the children like Cassandra, Josie and Art's foster daughter from England. But the remaining children in Britain couldn't escape the war. The program to ship them to North America had stopped after the sinking of the *City of Benares*, when only thirteen of the one hundred children on board had survived. Maybe the Atlantic would reopen as a means of escape when Adam and Eve succeeded against the Germans' code.

The clock on the wall ticked the minutes away. Tension tightened Mark's neck and shoulders until it felt like they would snap.

Then it happened.

Eve stopped.

Eve reversed.

Eve stopped again.

A cheer erupted as Admiral Meader walked toward Eve. Desch lurched to his feet and hurried to the printed story. He waved Mark over. "Run this through the Enigma."

Mark nodded and walked to the second Enigma. His heart pounded in anticipation. The Enigma would provide proof of their success—or failure. He turned the four wheels to match the settings on the story. A technician brought a message over and typed it into the Enigma. Meader read the paper tape as it slipped from the machine. Mark smiled as once again he thought he recognized some German words. Meader slapped him on the back.

"Gentlemen, we have a jackpot!"

six

The cold month of May had given way to June. But the routine of life as a WAVES could drive Evelyn crazy. She needed a change from sitting in the same chair, day after day, soldering rotors. She squirmed at the thought of listening as Charlotte read through another work break.

Yes, the work had value.

Admiral Meader had let them know Adam's one stop in the code had already paid for the project. Good. But she wanted more. She longed to be part of the program that led to more stops. The energy flowing beneath the surface that day had been electric. And she'd watched from the sidelines.

She didn't want to be a small cog in the larger project. While the project needed each little gear and piece to work, she felt cut out of the overall vision. Even Vivian looked at her with disapproval. Why couldn't she settle down and at least pretend contentment? While the other gals relished their breaks and having Charlotte read the next chapter to them, Evelyn itched to dash into the hall, find Mark, and ferret out what else happened while her fellow WAVES stayed locked in their isolated room.

"All right, ladies." Charlotte stood and clapped her hands. "Our day is done. Time to gather with the others for the walk home."

Evelyn joined the women at the door.

Would the WAVES have met her expectations if they'd taken the train all the way across the country to the West Coast?

No. The underlying restlessness stemmed from more than her position. Evelyn knew that as surely as she knew there would be no mail in her slot when she reached Sugar Camp.

She marched out of Building 26 with the other WAVES.

"What has you in a funk?" Lonnie strode next to her, marching in time with the others.

The orderly clump of hundreds of feet marching in time drilled into Evelyn's head, adding to the layer of tension pounding her head. "Not sure."

"Join us for dinner. I'm ready to spend time with friends." Vivian turned and grinned from her spot in front of Evelyn. "The kind that like to have fun." She waggled her eyebrows, and Evelyn laughed at the Groucho Marx impersonation.

As soon as they reached Sugar Camp, the three girls locked arms and hurried to the cafeteria. Evelyn allowed the other two to drag her to the mail area. While Vivian and Lonnie hurried forward to their slots, Evelyn hung back.

"Come on. You need to check, too." Lonnie fixed her sternest stare on Evelyn.

Evelyn shook her head. "There's no reason."

Vivian pouted. "Just because you haven't had mail yet doesn't mean today won't be your day."

"You don't know my family." Her father was entirely too busy to waste time contacting his only child. Government contacts would keep him in perpetual motion. And her mother would be actively engaged on the social circuit. When one was married to an industrial lobbyist, one must be seen. Letters to a daughter were not seen by the people who mattered. Maybe Evelyn was destined to live a life where the only safe expectations were those that never developed.

"Do you want me to check for you?" Lonnie's offer was sweet, but it wouldn't change anything.

Evelyn approached her slot. Just once. . .

She closed her eyes, took a breath, and reached into the slot. She felt nothing but the wooden sides. "See. Nothing." She forced a smile. "I really don't need to look to know there won't be mail."

Vivian's jaw had dropped, and Lonnie shuffled her feet.

Evelyn sniffed and stepped back. "I need to get something

from the cabin. See you guys at supper." She hurried from the building before they could see the tears. Maybe someday, the daily reminder that she didn't matter wouldn't hurt. Maybe.

That night, Evelyn made sure she buried her nose in a book whenever Lonnie or Viv looked ready to engage her. The next morning, she hurried from the cabin and into formation. She needed the anonymity of hiding in a sea of women.

The recent arrival of more WAVES made that easier, but it also indicated the program had accelerated in some way. While she wanted to hide, would the additions make it harder to stand out at NCR? Her skills made her unique from most, but she could be stuck with the mundane job of soldering rotors until the war ended. The thought killed her dreams. Maybe she should have followed her mother's advice and settled for a worthy occupation like nursing or teaching. Instead, she'd risked everything on a gamble to get her father's attention. Ironic, considering he'd be more likely to pay attention if she'd stayed in DC and married a society man.

After she lost count of which rotor she was on, a shadow settled over her.

"Hey, Evelyn."

Evelyn looked up to find Viv standing over her.

"Ready for lunch?"

"Can we leave Building 26?"

Viv laughed. "And go where?"

"Don't you think they have another cafeteria or two on this complex? Maybe the food's better." Evelyn wrinkled her nose. "Would you like Spam casserole or Spamloaf today?"

"You have a point."

Sometimes it felt like more than a railroad spur separated Building 26 from the rest of the NCR complex. Her stomach growled, and Evelyn laughed. "Guess I should settle for any food I find."

The two joined the other employees filtering into the cafeteria. After filling a plate with an egg salad sandwich and bowl of fruit, Evelyn found a table with two vacant seats. Viv settled into the chair across from her and took a bite of some sort of casserole Evelyn had avoided.

Viv pointed her fork at Evelyn. "Join us tomorrow? A group of us are taking a bus to Coney Island in Cincinnati."

"What's that?"

Viv grinned with a glint that worried Evelyn. "Join us, and you'll find out. Quit thinking so much, and come have some fun. All this work is making you a dull girl."

Evelyn took a drink of milk. "All right. I'll join you. Can I help with any of the details?" The last time Viv had planned an event, key details like transportation and meals got overlooked.

"I've got it covered." Viv wrinkled her nose. "That was a one-time occurrence."

"Are you certain? I'd hate to walk all the way to Cincinnati. Sure you don't need me to help?"

"Oh no you don't. I'm redeeming myself. Expect the time of your life." Viv flounced off to join a couple of WAVES at another table.

Evelyn watched her go and chuckled. Tomorrow would be an adventure.

❧

The next morning, Viv bounced Evelyn out of bed before the sun had crested over the horizon.

"Come on, Viv. This is my one morning to sleep in."

"Only because you're going to church with that local family."

She had a point. "Still. . ."

"If you're coming with us, you have to get out of bed, sleepyhead. The sun is up, and the bus will leave whether or not you're ready." Viv grabbed Evelyn's blanket and pulled it back. "Come on." She made a motion like she would tickle Evelyn out of bed.

Evelyn launched to her feet, laughing. "You've convinced me."

"Comes from growing up with oodles of siblings. You won't regret it."

Maybe not, but as she raced around her roommates to get

ready, Evelyn wondered how comfortable the bus trip from Dayton to Cincinnati would be. In a rush, a group of about eight WAVES piled into Sugar Camp's not-so-trusty woody station wagon.

"Are you sure Woody will last to the station?" Evelyn shifted to get someone's elbow out of her side.

Lonnie twisted awkwardly in the front passenger seat. "If not, we'll have a long walk ahead of us. Let's get this bucket of bolts on the road."

Virginia Jones sat behind the wheel and turned the key in the ignition. After a few stuttering attempts, the engine finally turned over. "Here we go."

Fifteen minutes later after some starts and stops, she pulled over near the bus stop. Evelyn stood in line with the others to get her ticket.

"There they are." Vivian's voice squeaked. "I didn't think they'd come."

Evelyn followed Viv's gaze and saw a group of men, some sailors and some civilians, headed their way. One or two had a girl with them, but all seemed eager to have a good time. Evelyn scanned the group. It added an interesting dynamic, and increased the outing's appeal. She'd kept her head down too much since arriving. Her gaze landed on Mark Miller— with a woman who looked like a movie starlet hanging on his arm. Paige?

❧

Mark had welcomed the chance to get up to Coney Island. Without Kat to nag him into taking her every other weekend, this might be his best chance. The summer was young, but with the hours work demanded, he couldn't expect more opportunities to get away to Cincinnati. Paige had jumped at the chance to accompany him and the Building 26 group.

He watched the blond beauty on his arm. She flitted beside him more than she walked, seeming to float with each step, a light touch on his arm.

She wore pants and a colorful blouse and had wrapped a

scarf around her hair. Paige shone like a ray of light amid the WAVES in their sports clothes, where most still tended to navy and white like their uniforms. Paige matched what he looked for in a woman. She was beautiful, active in the community and her church, and for some crazy reason liked him.

She must have felt his gaze, because Paige looked up at him. "Mark?"

"Mm-hmm?"

"Are you sure we need to go with the group? Wouldn't it be more fun to slip off by ourselves? I never get to spend time with you." Her voice purred against his neck.

Mark patted her hand but shook his head. "Not today. We'll have a great time with everyone."

"So..."

"Let's start with them, and we'll see what happens when we get to Coney Island. They invited us to join them, not dive off and do our own thing."

Her smile faltered, just at the corners. "Of course. You're right. Forgive me for being selfish."

Mark tightened his hold on her as someone bumped into them from behind. He glanced away and stumbled as his gaze met that of Evelyn Happ. She'd watched them. Caught some part of their exchange. Why did that bother him? She wasn't his vision of the ideal woman. Sure, she looked great, and she understood him and valued what he did in a way that Paige didn't even try to grasp. He stopped his thoughts from continuing down that path. He was here—wanted to be here—with Paige.

Evelyn had an underlying desire for her life to matter, to have a purpose. He'd seen it when she didn't know it leaked out. Sometimes at church, he glimpsed the wariness mixed with yearning.

No, he wouldn't think about her. While she'd joined his family for church and lunch several Sundays, she'd made it clear she wasn't a Christian. As much as he prayed for her, he'd promised himself he'd allow himself to imagine a lifetime relationship only with someone who had committed her life to Christ. He turned to Paige and listened as she talked about her week teaching first-graders.

≈

Evelyn tried to ignore the envy that cropped up as she watched Mark with his girl. He seemed engrossed in every word she said. Evelyn couldn't remember the last time a man had given her that kind of attention. Instead, when she was with men, they'd either wanted to test her engineering ability or keep her entertained with a movie or dance.

Even that hadn't happened in a while.

What would it be like to be a porcelain beauty like Mark's Paige? She'd never know.

She had two choices: mope or ignore it. Ignoring it sounded much more enjoyable. Especially as a damp breeze tickled her hair across her face as she boarded the bus filled with eligible men. Setting her face away from Mark Miller and the promise he represented but could never fulfill, Evelyn turned to the closest seaman and engaged him in conversation. She'd been so frustrated with her WAVES assignment she hadn't realized how isolated she'd let herself become. She wasn't normally a wallflower, and as she bantered with her fellow travelers, she felt more like herself. In no time, she had the men and WAVES in the seats around her laughing. When they reached the park, she had a man on each arm urging her to join him.

Viv caught her eye and frowned. Evelyn glanced around and understood. Looked like she couldn't keep two to herself or one of the other gals would travel solo. Not the right approach if she wanted to maintain friendships.

Instead of pairing off, the group stayed together and tried out the various roller coasters and other rides. A smaller group opted to spend the afternoon at the swimming pool, but Evelyn hadn't made the trip to do something she could do at Sugar Camp. She raced from ride to ride, determined to squeeze as many as possible into the few precious free hours. After one too many sodas mixed with cotton candy, her stomach churned, and she laughingly shooed the others toward another ride. She watched them board a car and started to sit on a bench. Instead, she eased onto something soft.

"Ack!" Evelyn jumped up, hand over her heart.

"I can move," a deep voice intoned.

Heat rushed into her cheeks. "I am so sorry." She couldn't look at him.

Mark tugged her hand. "There's room for two. Come on. Sit down."

Evelyn eased next to him, ready to leap to her feet if there wasn't sufficient room. She settled against the wood slats of the bench and cleared her throat. "Where's your date?"

"She decided to rest by the pool." Mark shrugged. "I'd rather watch the fun here. Want to hop on the next car?"

Evelyn looked at the Wildcat, and her stomach rebelled at the thought of the turns and plunges. "How about the Ferris wheel? That's more my speed at this point."

"All right."

They walked side by side across the park. Mark shoved his hands in his pockets. Evelyn tried to keep her gaze in front of her but watched him instead. He seemed content to walk quietly, while she—tempted to fill the silence with words—bit the inside of her cheek to restrain her chattering.

"How do you like the life of a WAVES?"

She considered the question a moment. "What I should have expected. How do you like being an engineer?"

He stopped and looked at her, eyes sparkling. "More some days than others."

"Depending on if the Bombes cooperate?"

His expression closed, and he warily scanned the people around them. "Be careful, Evelyn."

"You're right." She didn't want to end up in some hospital for the rest of the war because she spoke without thinking. "Do you ever feel trapped by expectations?"

"That's an odd question." He purchased tickets for the ride and handed one to her. "I focus on solving problems. My supervisors expect me to solve problems, and I want to keep them happy."

"I suppose."

They settled into one of the ride's cars. The attendant pulled the bar down in front of them. Trying not to brush against Mark, Evelyn looked out across the river as the Ferris wheel started turning.

Mark seemed content to take in the view. "What do you see when you look at the rides?"

"Marvels of engineering designed to give us thrills as we ride them, while hopefully maintaining safety."

"Know what I see?"

Evelyn shook her head.

"I see laws that were established by a Creator who carefully constructed the world and everything in it. Only a mind so much bigger than anything we could do as humans could create the layers of complexity, then reveal the underlying simplicity to human minds to break down and build on. I think that also demonstrates His concern and love for humans. To think of the myriad complications and details and design them in a way to provide for our needs." He shook his head. "It's amazing and humbling."

The ride ended, and they stepped off.

"There you are." A sugary sweet voice made Mark turn. "I wondered where I'd find you, Mark."

"Thanks for the company, Evelyn." Mark put his arm around Paige's shoulder. "I bet it's time to head back to the bus."

The look Paige shot toward Evelyn made it clear the woman believed she hadn't shown up a moment too soon.

Evelyn watched them walk toward the parking lot. Thoughtfully, she looked up, absorbing the sight of multiple rides constructed of wonderful, whirring wheels and gears, now laced with sparkling lights, outlining them against the darkening sky. What if Mark was right?

Someone or something had engineered the underlying rules that she studied and entrusted her life to. Despite conversations with people like Mark and his mother and the occasional visit to church as a child, she didn't understand the complexities of God. She knew the Christmas and Easter stories. Kind of. Maybe it was time to try to break the code. Begin to understand the faith of those she admired. Determine whether God cared about her and her frustrations.

seven

Adam and Eve had made successful runs but still hadn't achieved the consistency the navy demanded. Mark wrestled with the problem on his walk to NCR and returned to the same conclusion no matter which angle he used. The group needed fresh eyes. The thought wasn't new to him. In fact, he'd gotten quite adept at avoiding it, but that didn't change the facts.

The only person he could think to bring into the project was Evelyn Happ, an unsettling proposition.

But why should it matter if the person who might bring a fresh perspective to the project was a woman? As his mother continued to invite Evelyn over for Sunday church and dinner, he'd gotten to know her, a fact Paige didn't appreciate. But what could he do? Order his mother to end her friendship with Evelyn? That wasn't right. If Paige was nervous, maybe she should spend her Sundays at church with him and come to dinner, too. He hadn't thought that attending different churches was a problem. Maybe he was wrong.

No, Paige overreacted. Evelyn was smart and savvy. He'd seen how quickly her mind worked as she debated his father on all things biblical. The woman seemed determined to examine everything she learned from as many angles as possible. While she still appeared reluctant to accept a relationship with Christ, he prayed her eyes would open. And that it wouldn't affect her ability to analyze the machines.

The only reason not to mention her ability was pride. Such an ugly word. One he didn't like slapping on himself. But what else could he think? At core, he didn't want to risk a woman finding the solution to the Bombe problem.

He opened the doors and walked into Building 26. After passing through the layers of security, he reached Adam's room, ready to get to work. Then he saw her.

"There's a problem with overheating." No hello or other greeting from Evelyn Happ. Straight to the heart of the issue.

How had she worked her way back into the room? He opened the door, checked for the MP. Yep, there he was. "How did you get in here?"

"Walked in like you." She relaxed in a chair, one shapely ankle laced on top of the other. How could a woman make a uniform look that eye-catching? Mark averted his gaze. "Let's focus on the issue."

"The issue is that you aren't supposed to be here."

"No." She placed her feet on the floor and stared at him. "It's overheating. You're working the machines too hard."

"Any first-year engineering student would deduce that." John glared at her, arms crossed and brows drawn together.

Evelyn dipped her chin in acknowledgment. "But why? What's causing it?"

"Believe me, we've applied the scientific method backward and forward to this problem. If there was an explanation, we'd have it."

"Calm down, John." Mark turned toward the woman. "Have any thoughts you'd care to share on how to fix the overheating?"

"Not yet." She chewed on her lip a moment. "How many RPMs is it supposed to cycle?"

"Too many."

She cocked an eyebrow at him. So she didn't like the fact he glossed over actual numbers. Too bad. He wouldn't say another word until he knew she had clearance.

"So what would you like me to do? Since you won't let me engineer the problem?"

"I don't know. If you'll excuse us." Mark turned his back on her and focused on the machine.

"You are an infuriating man."

"That's what my sisters tell me all the time." This reinforced the point that they needed to get her assigned to the room or moved out of Dayton. No matter how she accomplished it, she couldn't keep breaching security. The ease with which she did so made him wonder who else might be able to break in. "Evelyn—"

"Ensign Happ."

Fine. "Ensign Happ, you need to leave."

"Yes, sir. I'll head back to the completely mindless work of soldering rotors."

"It's important work. Without those rotors constructed properly, Adam and Eve and the other machines couldn't operate."

"I know that." Her words snapped into the space between them as she poked a finger into his chest. "Don't treat me like an imbecile."

He stepped back, unsure what she would say or do next.

She deflated, pulling in on herself. "I'm sorry." She took a deep breath. "You're right that carefully crafting those rotors is an incredibly important part of the process." She turned to leave. "But anyone could do that job. They don't need an engineering background. It would probably be better if they didn't."

Mark shoved his hands in his pockets so that he wouldn't reach out to comfort her. "I'm sorry, Ensign."

She waved his words away and continued to the door. "Try soaking the seals in oil."

"What?"

"I said, try soaking the seals in oil before installing them. That should cause the material to swell and prevent future oil leaks." She slipped into the hallway without looking back.

Mark turned to John. "Do you think?"

"Certainly doesn't hurt to try. I'll hunt for supplies right now."

"No time like the present to test a theory." And if they could actually stop the oil leaks or reduce the number, Evelyn would have proved her worth.

&

Evelyn had begun to believe the day would never end. After the humiliating episode in Adam's room, she'd slunk to her assigned room as her colleagues wandered in, quiet chatter indicating a readiness to tackle the day.

She needed to stop. She'd pushed too hard, and if she wasn't careful, she'd be shipped out of the navy. Her days at NCR should be spent like those of the other WAVES: focused on a specific task that might not seem important on its own, but when added to all the other pieces, it created an important whole.

Time to stop forcing her luck and accept her lot.

At the close of the day, the WAVES followed their familiar pattern and marched four abreast along Main Street back to Sugar Camp. A Model A roadster eased past them, overloaded with navy enlisted men calling out cadence. Evelyn ignored them along with the other honks and whistles from the stopped cars. She was more than ready to stop feeling like an oddity, a curiosity on the streets of Dayton.

But as she ignored everything else, her thoughts cycled like ruthless rebels back to her failed attempt. And to think throwing out a trite possibility to solve the oil leak problem would make a difference. Surely, those men had thought of and tried it. The suggestion had likely only made her look more foolish than her vain effort to sneak into the room.

She should be glad she didn't have to work in that noisy, sweltering room day after day. Soldering might be stationary, repetitive work, but at least she didn't hear the noise pounding in her mind long after her day ended.

Who did she think she was that she could solve problems that had plagued some of the brightest minds in the country for months?

What had her grandmama always said? Something like pride comes before the fall?

If today was any indication, her pride in her abilities had led to yet another fall. Sometime she should choose to do it when Mark Miller wasn't around. It didn't help that she'd see him again on Sunday. It wasn't like she had to join his family, but she enjoyed her time with Mr. and Mrs. Miller. She even appreciated getting to know Mark outside of Building 26's strictly controlled environment.

His family had something special, something that felt like coming home every time they welcomed her. So different from the formal atmosphere in her own home. She didn't want to believe it stemmed from their faith, but that, too, seemed genuine and real to the very core of each Miller. Though she could tell it wasn't their intention, their openness about their faith unsettled her.

No matter how she challenged him, Mark had a ready answer for every question she asked.

How could she know there was a God? Just look at creation. Could anything as complex and multi-dependent as creation simply spring into being without intentional thought and amazing creativity and wisdom? Despite his Ferris wheel speech, she wasn't sure.

She'd asked him, if God existed, why would He care about her? His answer? Because He chooses to. Mark had taken her to the Bible and shown her the early chapters in Genesis. The story of God creating everything and saying it was good. Of walking with the first two people. Evelyn wasn't sure she accepted the simplistic story, but the thought that a God who had created the world would choose to walk on it with His very creation amazed her.

It also consumed her thoughts in the quiet of the night.

What would it be like to know a love like that?

And how could that very same love turn its back on its own Son?

The WAVES passed through the main gate at Sugar Camp.

"Evelyn, join us for the movie in the auditorium tonight." Lonnie pulled her along as the formation broke apart.

"What's showing?"

"Some second-run movie from last year or something.

Does it really matter? Let's stay out of our room for a bit. Relax with some of the other gals before the whole process repeats tomorrow." Lonnie spoke with an earnestness that kept Evelyn from laughing.

"All right. Just make sure Viv and Mary Ellen know what we're up to. I won't have anyone feeling slighted."

A bubbly laugh surrounded Evelyn. She turned to find Viv behind her.

"You're the one we're worried about." Viv pulled her hat off. "You know I'm up for a night of not thinking."

"I thought that pretty much described our days."

Lonnie sighed. "Unlike you, Evelyn, the rest of us are pretty content to do what the navy tells us to and forget about it the moment we leave Building 26. There is more to life, you know. Even if that more includes a movie."

Mary Ellen walked up. "Movie? I hope this one includes Cary Grant."

"I'm hoping for James Cagney." Viv pretended to swoon while Lonnie caught her.

"You are too much." Evelyn laughed, glad to leave her worries behind her. "I prefer Humphrey Bogart. Maybe *Casablanca*."

"That film?" Lonnie rolled her eyes. "I can't see anyone liking it. It's so dreary. Why would Rick let Ilsa go? No, give me a real man like Jimmy Stewart."

The banter continued as the women changed into play clothes and headed to the auditorium. Lonnie shrieked when the credits rolled showing the film of the evening was *Philadelphia Story*. Evelyn grinned at Viv and Mary Ellen, and the three promptly fell into mock swoons. Lonnie frowned at them.

"Looks like you and Mary Ellen can both be happy. Viv and I will have to pretend we're seeing our leading men." Evelyn tried to focus on the antics of the socialite and her two beaus, and it worked. . .most of the time.

※

The next morning, Evelyn slipped into her assigned room in

Building 26, prepared to settle in and make the most of her assignment. It might not be much, but she would try her best to focus on doing the job well. Especially since she had no other choice.

Charlotte Johnson walked toward Evelyn's seat, a furrow knit into her brow. "Evelyn, I'm not sure what's going on, but Admiral Meader has asked to see you in his office." She kept her voice low, but even so, Evelyn noticed a couple of the WAVES shift in their seats.

"Thank you." Evelyn stood, a sudden swirl of nausea assaulting her. She pressed a hand against her stomach and swallowed. Maybe this was it. Maybe he was ready to send her home or to St. Elizabeth's for pushing her way into Adam's room.

When she reached his office, she announced herself to his secretary. A moment later, the sailor ushered her into his office. Evelyn stopped when she saw Mr. Desch and Mark in the room. Mark smiled, an act which slowed her pulse a trifle. But why would the three want to see her?

"Ensign Happ, please have a seat." Admiral Meader watched her closely.

"Yes, sir." She eased onto the edge of the seat.

"It has come to my attention you are intent on joining the group engineering our machines."

"Yes, sir."

"Why is that?" He leaned forward, elbows planted on his desk.

Evelyn worried her lower lip a moment. How should she answer the question? "I believe I can contribute to the project."

"How?"

She looked at Mark, but he gave no indication where these questions would lead. "I have an engineering degree from Purdue University. I bring a fresh perspective to the machines and may identify solutions and fixes."

"You think our work has been sloppy?"

"No, sir." Evelyn leaned forward until she almost reached

his desk. "From the little I've seen of the machines, I think your team has done amazing work." She took a deep breath. If they sent her home after this, there was nothing she could do about that. "I also know that Adam and the other machines still aren't working the way you and Mr. Desch expect and need. I haven't been here through the stages of development. I won't be weighed down by knowledge that this or that has been tried in the past and didn't work."

Admiral Meader held up a hand. "You've convinced me. More than that, your approach to the oil leaks shows me you should be given an opportunity."

Evelyn felt like her heart had stopped. Did he just say an opportunity? She sought Mark, and he nodded slightly. He'd told them her suggestion? She wanted to leap to her feet and hug him, them shriek. Instead, she remained rooted in her chair and tried not to grin like an overeager child.

"Thank you, sir."

"Don't thank me until you hear the extent of your focus."

eight

Evelyn walked into Adam's room on June 18, wondering what the day would bring. Getting transferred from her old assignment to engineering hadn't resulted in the excitement and sense of contribution she'd expected. While she now sat in Adam's room, she often had to insert herself into the conversations, an exercise that left her drained. She wanted to participate as an equal with the men.

Instead, she watched someone else turn on the machine. If they were lucky, the machine cooperated and ran for a while. If the day was really good, the machine might hit, leading to a jackpot. If the day was a bad one, the machine would break down and take hours to repair.

The challenge was the troubleshooting.

The delicate Bombes liked to break down when under the pressure of the high-speed runs. Then there was the time needed to set them up. It took precision work to get the rotors set properly. She hadn't seen the process, but Evelyn surmised someone somewhere had narrowed down the possible combinations. Otherwise, it would be impossible to know where to start with the billions of potential combinations.

Mark approached her as she placed her purse and hat on top of a file cabinet. "Have you heard?"

"Heard what?" What was it with engineers releasing information in dribs and drabs? Or was that the military influence?

Mark rubbed his head, tenting his hands behind his head. "The navy sent a memo to Desch, ordering him to scrap the Bombes and start over."

"Start over?" Evelyn couldn't imagine doing that. She looked at Adam and the work it represented. "And lose all the hours and improvements you've made? That doesn't make sense, even for the military. What possible reason do they have for ordering that?"

"That's the question, sister." John Fields pulled a chair up and straddled it.

Mark collapsed in the chair next to John. "The brass are infatuated with an electronic machine. It's déjà vu."

Evelyn looked between the two men. Both appeared lost in a fog of disillusionment.

"Didn't we already go through this?" John crossed his arms across the chair's back. "There's nothing we can do to design and build an electronic machine under their constraints."

"You'll have to catch me up. What's the basic problem with this machine?"

John started to give her a come-on look, so she hurried to add, "Beyond breaking down."

"There isn't a problem if we can get it to work consistently." Mark shrugged. "The key problem? The machine is unreliable, and that's unacceptable to the navy."

"But designing a new one will take months."

"Not the way they see it. The original due date for delivery of the machines holds."

Evelyn took the last chair. No wonder the men were so upset. The navy wanted the impossible. "Has it been like this the whole time? Moving targets and changes?"

Mark nodded. "See why we're worn out?"

"Yes." Time to break down the problem. "The oil leaks are under control."

"Well, better since we've soaked the seals."

"What about the rotors?"

"Still skip contacts."

They had to rectify that problem before Adam could work reliably. "Let's focus there."

John guffawed. "Why bother? It's all getting killed by the navy anyway."

"With an attitude like that, maybe. But we can find the

solution if we look. That's what I intend to do. You and the rest have spent too much time on this to scrap it now." Evelyn looked at Mark. Would he agree with her or side with John? She didn't know enough about the project at this stage to troubleshoot herself. A thoughtful look cloaked his face.

She needed the help.

The door banged open, and Desch marched in. "You've heard."

Evelyn nodded along with the two men.

"Don't sit there; we've got work to do. I am not about to follow the memo unless there is absolutely no option. The technology isn't ready to produce what those men in Washington demand." The intense look in Desch's eyes left no doubt they'd spend hours today on the hunt for a solution.

Other than when Desch went to the admiral's office to argue his case, the group worked together. Evelyn's pulse raced as ideas and analysis flowed. For once, she experienced what she'd longed for. She was functioning as part of a group engineering an important problem that required her expertise.

If they found a solution, this might turn into the best day of her life.

&

Mark watched Evelyn as they threw out ideas. Some were terrible, but others had merit. The problem was they didn't have the time to cover old ground.

Desch had them pull out each component and scrutinize it.

"What are we looking for?" Evelyn's words whispered uncomfortably close to his neck.

He slid a bit to the side and shrugged. "We'll know it when we see it."

"I've always hated that statement. So unhelpful."

"But sometimes it's the truth."

She dipped her head in agreement. "You've got a point. Doesn't make it any easier, though." She sighed and rubbed her forehead as if a headache gathered beneath the skin.

Admiral Meader strode into the room. He surveyed the

parts strewn over the surfaces. "Find anything?"

Desch shook his head. "Not yet. But we will. We've got some of the brightest minds in this country working on the problem."

"That's not good enough, Joe." Meader sighed. "I've talked to my superiors. Their position hasn't changed. This design of yours isn't working so they want to move on."

"And waste millions of dollars and all the invested man-hours?"

"They want to stop the bleeding."

Mark looked at Evelyn out of the corner of his eye. She shifted in her seat and fumbled with her hair, brushing it behind her ears. If he had to guess, she wanted to be anywhere but here. Did her hair feel as soft as it looked?

Desch stared at Admiral Meader like he'd gone crazy, and Mark didn't blame him one bit. Desch turned red. "The navy wants us to scrap the Bombe design? Start over? Just like that?"

The admiral nodded, back stiff as a ramrod. "I got you twenty-four hours to find an alternative."

Twenty-four hours? It felt like a grenade had exploded in the room, killing everything Mark had invested his life in this last year. Desch stared through Meader as if ignoring the man's existence.

Evelyn twisted her fingers in her lap, her gaze bouncing back and forth between the two men and the machine. She mouthed, *What do we do now?*

Mark shrugged. That was the question of the hour.

Hours later, he dragged himself home. They hadn't found the silver bullet, but they'd run out of ideas. Desch had sent them off to get a few hours sleep before trying again in the morning.

His mother met him in the hallway, a letter in her hand.

"Good evening, Mother."

"A rough day?" She pulled her robe tight at her neck.

Mark tossed his hat on the rack and smoothed his hair. "You could say that."

"I have a plate in the warming oven for you." She handed

the letter to him, the creases around her eyes cut deep. "This came today. From the draft board."

As if the day hadn't been frustrating enough. "Wonder what this is about. Maybe they'd like to ship me to Antarctica again."

"Sarcasm doesn't become you."

Maybe not, but it made an impossible situation somewhat tenable. No, she was right. A mom's prerogative. "Sorry." He flipped the envelope over. Another summons to come before the board. Explain why he shouldn't be shipped overseas. It should be a simple matter to get his II-A or II-B status, since he was needed for his job. But the board didn't see it that way. Nope, and the top-secret nature of the project made it impossible to explain why he had to stay in Dayton.

The thought of facing those dour-faced men again was like adding lemon to an already bitter day. He didn't know if he could stomach it.

Scanning the letter, Mark discovered he'd have to show up at three o'clock tomorrow afternoon or the police would come for him. Life would be so much easier if the navy would give him some kind of exemption from service. He served but in a way invisible to most of the population. In particular, the draft board.

"Don't worry, Mom. Everything's fine." His stomach growled, bringing a smile to Mom's face. "I think I'll eat that food now."

≈

The next morning, the engineers raced against the steadily moving hands of the clock. If he had to guess, Mark would say Desch never made it home.

"Gentlemen—and lady—" Desch nodded at Evelyn, who colored. "We're looking at this problem from an incorrect perspective." He marched back and forth across the room. "You're focused on the theories of engineering. That's all well and good most days. Right now, however, we must apply those theories to the practical world. While all theories indicate these machines should work, reality is that they don't. What practically could cause that?"

John shrugged. "Heat from the RPMs required."

"Certainly, but we've examined that. There's little to nothing we can do about that. What else? Ensign Happ?"

Evelyn swallowed as her gaze raced across the machine. Mark could almost see her mind racing through calculations and maneuvers in her attempt to find a solution. "Sir, I'd consider whether the individual parts withstand the intense pressure exerted against them."

"A worthy objective. Miller?"

"Maybe the problem is with the contacts. Something getting in between the connections and preventing the electrical impulses."

Desch quirked an eyebrow at him. "Nice piggyback to Ensign Happ's suggestion."

The door opened and Admiral Meader strode in. He thrust a paper at Desch. "I've convinced the bigwigs in Washington to proceed with your design. Too much time, money, and manpower wasted otherwise. They're going along. For now. Get these machines working and the production models ready to transport. We still need those on the train to Washington by July 15." The man turned and left without waiting for a response. The weight of imminent failure departed with him.

"Looks like we have a reprieve, but it's only that." Desch turned back to the machine, his pipe poking out of the corner of his mouth. "We have work to do. Back at it."

A bit before three o'clock, Mark slipped out of Building 26 and headed to his draft board appointment. He'd heard tales from colleagues about being escorted to the train station by military police to ensure they boarded the train to their appointments with various boot camps. At the last moment, Joe Desch or someone else from Building 26 had shown up with a letter of some sort and snatched them back to NCR. Mark had avoided such theatrics, but would his luck hold?

Maybe it was time to serve in uniform. Occasionally as he read the paper or listened to news reports from the front, he wondered if what he did truly mattered.

Would the war be better served if he went to boot camp and wherever the army assigned him? Yet the project at Building 26 was important. The navy presence and security made that clear, even if he never knew the full extent of its value.

If he didn't fully understand the project, he couldn't expect to make the draft board understand. Especially with the vow of secrecy he'd taken. The navy left no doubt he'd be shot if he breathed a word about the true nature of his work.

Mark trudged the last block to the meeting and squared his shoulders. He couldn't go into the meeting weighed down by uncertainty. *Father, You're in charge of this. Continue to guide me in the steps You have for me.*

The unsettled boulders resting on his shoulders slowly lifted. Okay, now he could proceed in peace.

Mark walked up to the reception desk. A harried man looked at him, frost in his eyes.

"Mark Miller here for a three o'clock appointment."

"Yes." The man shuffled a few files. "They're waiting for you. Follow me."

Inside the room, four men sat behind a table littered with stacks of teetering files. Mark nodded at them, then sat on the only open chair in front of them. He wondered if he should hunker down for potshots as he waited for the proceeding to start.

A tall man in the middle, dressed in a dapper suit with gold watch attached to his pocket, stared at him. Mark resisted the urge to squirm under the examination.

"Young man, you appear entirely capable of walking without assistance."

"Yes."

"You do not require a medical waiver?"

"No, sir."

"Yet you have not reported for service. You have no

dependents to prevent service. You have not requested conscientious-objector status. I fail to see why we shouldn't escort you to the next train."

"As I stated at my appointment last year, my job is of a sensitive nature and requires my presence."

"You work at the National Cash Register Company."

"Yes, sir."

"I am not aware of any projects that prohibit eligible young men from performing their patriotic duty." The man looked at his colleagues, who nodded their agreement. Mark swallowed around a dry throat, visions of an armed guard taking him to boot camp filling his mind.

"I wish I could tell you more, but I can't."

"Why not?" The man leaned forward, a frown etched on his face.

"Because I've taken an oath that prohibits me from discussing the particulars of my job and responsibilities with anyone. Even my coworkers."

"That is patently unbelievable. We are in Dayton, not some top-secret, secure location." The man narrowed his eyes. "Will you report to the train station on Monday morning for transport to basic training?"

Mark closed his eyes. This wasn't going as he'd hoped when he'd prayed, but he had only one answer. "No, sir."

"Then you will spend the weekend in jail until you are escorted there."

A soldier stepped to his side. "If you'll follow me." While posed as a request, the gun at the man's side and the firmness in his stance made it clear Mark had no choice.

"Do I get a phone call?"

The man grunted. "We'll see if we can arrange that."

Mark followed the man into the hallway, a sinking sensation in his gut. If something didn't happen, he'd be on his way to who knew where. He had to get a call out.

nine

Sunday morning when the Millers picked Evelyn up, Mark didn't fill half the backseat. Instead, Marjorie looked pasty and Mr. Miller greeted her with an unusually solemn expression.

Evelyn slid into the backseat. "Is Mark ill?"

"No." Marjorie's words fell heavy in the car. "He hasn't come home since he left for work on Friday."

That didn't seem like something the oh-so-responsible Mark Miller would do. "He left work early but didn't mention anything."

"He had a meeting with the draft board. We haven't heard from him or seen him since."

"Has this happened before?"

Mr. Miller nodded. "Yes, but he's always explained that his job at NCR requires him to stay in town. It's worked so far."

"Doesn't the navy do anything? Seems they should since he works for them."

"The navy hasn't. And since he can't explain his job, nobody on the board understands it. You know more about what he does than we do, Evelyn." Mr. Miller shrugged, but it looked like the burden he carried settled on his shoulders rather than eased. "Everything's so hush-hush I couldn't do anything to help him even if I knew where they kept him."

Marjorie wiped her eyes with a delicate handkerchief. "I'm sorry we aren't better company."

"Please don't apologize. If today isn't a good day, I will understand."

Mr. Miller turned into the Christ Community Church parking lot. Marjorie leaned back over the seat. "Please don't think that. I have looked forward to spending today with you. A ray of sunlight in a dreary weekend."

Evelyn nodded, then slipped from the car and followed the Millers into the sanctuary. People filled the fellowship area with quiet conversation, that of friends reconnecting after a week apart. The warmth of the interactions still caught Evelyn off guard. No artifice existed among the members of the small congregation. Instead, they cared about each other in a way that Evelyn wanted to experience. After several weeks joining the Millers, she judged the interest and concern in each other's lives genuine. She'd keep watching but thought she might want to become part of something that real.

Person after person inquired about Mark. Marjorie answered quietly, but her posture collapsed a bit more with each kind question.

Evelyn slipped up to her side. "Should we go find a seat in the sanctuary?"

"I think our pew will be there as usual."

"You might need the break from all the concern."

With a wry laugh, Marjorie nodded. "I suppose you're right." She sighed. "There's nothing I can do for Mark by talking. Only prayer can help now."

Evelyn followed Marjorie to their usual pew. Marjorie could pray. Evelyn would visit the Desches, make sure Mr. Desch knew the draft board had one of his engineers. Surely he could do something.

The congregation stood to sing a hymn. Evelyn shared a hymnal with Marjorie but listened rather than join in the singing. Familiar words welled in the sanctuary:

> *Amazing grace! How sweet the sound*
> *That saved a wretch like me!*
> *I once was lost, but now am found;*
> *Was blind, but now I see.*

The words were no clearer now than when she'd first heard them as a child. Sitting through services for several weeks hadn't helped unlock the meaning. Why sing about grace? Wasn't being good sufficient? Why would anyone need grace if they lived a life of service and adhered to society's laws and mores?

Merely sitting in the church hadn't helped. The pastor seemed intent on communicating truth to his congregation, but Evelyn still didn't understand the grave importance everyone put on his words. The Millers clearly lived in accordance with the teachings of their church. But did it make a difference?

The thoughts made her head ache. She shook her head slightly to clear it. If the questions returned, she'd entertain them. For now, though, she'd focus on Mark. His parents had welcomed her as one of their own. The least she could do was work to secure his return.

On the drive to the Millers' home, Marjorie turned to watch her. "What did you think of the sermon, Evelyn?"

"I'm not sure."

Marjorie quirked an eyebrow at her.

"I was distracted."

"By thoughts of my fine-looking son." Mr. Miller winked at her through the rearview mirror.

"Louis!" Mrs. Miller playfully slapped his shoulder. "I apologize for my husband."

Evelyn laughed and felt a release of tension. "He's fine. And actually, yes, your son did distract me from whatever thoughts the pastor attempted to share with us. I'm afraid I wasn't an attentive listener."

"Here we are, ladies." Mr. Miller parked the car.

"Come help me, Evelyn. Lunch will only take a moment to prepare."

Evelyn followed Marjorie back to the kitchen. The windows in the room opened to a view of the landscaped backyard. Marjorie's victory garden filled the back third of the yard, a project Evelyn's mother would assign to one of the staff. "Looks like the garden is doing well."

"Yes. You can help me harvest some of it next week. The

beans are getting close." Marjorie slipped on an apron. "Do you enjoy coming to church with us? The reason I ask is I don't want to force you to join us if you'd rather not."

Taking a moment to consider, Evelyn nodded. "I appreciate attending with you. I can't say I understand everything."

"You'd be an exceptional person if you did. I've attended church my whole life and still find much to learn or a fresh way of looking at something. Our pastor is good at highlighting passages in a new way."

"Why does it matter?"

Marjorie looked at her quizzically and handed her a bowl of peas to snap.

"I mean, why does it make a difference whether you go to church or not?" Evelyn picked up a pea and snapped off the ends.

Pulling a meatloaf from the oven to set, Marjorie grabbed two glasses from the cupboard and filled them with water. "It's not the going to church that matters. It's the relationship with Jesus Christ that makes all the difference. I go to church to be encouraged in my faith and challenged to live in a manner that pleases Christ."

Evelyn considered her words. "But what makes Jesus so special? Each week the pastor invites people to give their lives to Him, but why bother?"

"Do you believe there is a God?"

"I suppose."

"Supposing isn't enough." Marjorie gestured out the window. "What do you see when you look in my backyard?"

"An abundance of plants you care for."

"Who made them?"

"Nobody. They just are."

Marjorie cocked her head, crossed her arms, and studied Evelyn. "Really? With all your scientific training, you believe something as complex as a tomato plant simply came to be?"

"The alternative is to believe that something created everything."

"Why would that be harder to believe than spontaneous evolution?"

Evelyn thought a moment. "I guess because your perspective requires faith."

"As does yours."

The quick rejoinder set Evelyn back. "I don't understand."

"No person observed creation. But neither did any person observe this 'just coming to be' that you accept."

Could Marjorie be right? "What does this have to do with Jesus?"

"The Bible tells us that Jesus is the Word of God. God spoke everything into existence through His Word. And Jesus came to die for the sins of the creation He made."

"Why? That doesn't make sense. If He's God, why die for others?"

"Because of love." Marjorie handed Evelyn a glass of water. A comfortable silence settled between them, as Evelyn weighed the words.

"I don't think I've known anyone who loved enough to lay down their life for their enemies." Evelyn shook her head as she tried to fathom that kind of love. "I'll have to think about that."

Marjorie nodded. "It's humbling to think the God of the universe, the Creator of everything, deemed you valuable enough to die for. If you want to explore this, read Genesis 1–3 and the book of John. There you'll find the evidence for what I mentioned."

"I'll do that."

In a few moments, they had the table set for dinner, and Mr. Miller joined them. After the meal was cleaned up, Evelyn slipped away, but not before Marjorie pressed a Bible into her hands.

"Read it if you're curious."

"Thank you." Evelyn carried the volume as she walked up the hill to Sugar Camp. When she arrived, she saw that Woody, the station wagon, sat in its parking slip. She signed out the keys and drove the vehicle to the Desches' home. Once there, she knocked on the door and waited for an answer.

Mrs. Desch opened the door. "Hello."

"Could I speak with Mr. Desch, please? It's about one of his men."

Mrs. Desch stepped back and motioned Evelyn into the home. "I'll go get him."

Admiral Meader walked around the corner. "Ensign Happ, what are you doing here?"

"I have a matter to discuss with Mr. Desch."

"I'm sure anything you have for him can be shared with me."

Evelyn stood at ease. "I'll have to let him decide since this involves a civilian, sir."

"Has the man broken your heart?" Merriment danced in Admiral Meader's eyes. "I'll be happy to assuage any unhappiness."

"No, thank you, sir." She wanted to shake her head. Admiral Meader's reputation with the ladies might be well-founded, after all.

Mr. Desch walked into the room. "Ensign Happ, what can I do for you?"

"I'm sorry to bother you at home, sir. However, I wanted to make sure you knew Mark Miller had a meeting with the draft board on Friday afternoon and has not returned home since. His parents are concerned the board is sending him out on Monday's train, sir."

Mr. Desch rubbed a hand across his forehead. "Admiral, this is exactly why we require papers releasing my men from the draft."

"I can't do that without jeopardizing the project."

Evelyn stepped back. Should she witness this conversation?

"Well, the project will be jeopardized if I lose the minds required to make the project successful."

"You think Miller wouldn't contribute to the war as a soldier?"

"I'm sure he'd make a fine soldier, but his talent would be wasted." Mr. Desch looked at Evelyn. "Thank you for alerting me to the situation." He glanced at Admiral Meader. "I'll see what I can do."

"Good afternoon, sir. Admiral." Evelyn turned to leave, uncomfortable at staying as the men continued to argue. She hadn't realized how tense things were between the two. And the admiral lived there? So much for Mr. Desch's home being his castle. And to think she thought the Revolutionary War had been fought in part to ensure the military wasn't quartered in private homes.

❧

Monday morning, Mark stood at Union Station, surrounded on both sides by military police. He tried to think of something to say to the men but decided there was no use. They merely followed orders and wouldn't have the clout to reverse the draft board's decision. Without a phone call, he hadn't alerted Desch or anyone else to his status. All he could do was go along.

He'd fight after all. Maybe he'd learn to hit something smaller than a shed. He'd have to, or he'd be the world's lousiest soldier.

Funny that, as the war erupted in Europe and spread to the Pacific, he'd never considered himself eligible to fight. He wasn't soldier material.

Guess he'd get to prove he could do it. And he'd have to excel at it like he had his studies at MIT.

"This is our train, Mr. Miller." The sailor to his right took a step toward the train.

"Where are we headed?"

"Chicago."

All right. The big city. They must think he should be in the navy. Ironic, considering he'd dedicated the last year of his life to a top-secret navy project. Even here, he'd keep his vow of secrecy. He'd rather fight than be shot for treason.

"All aboard." The conductor stepped onto the platform.

"After you, sir." The sailor waved him toward the car.

"Mr. Miller."

Mark turned to find the source of the voice. It sounded vaguely like Desch, but he had no reason to be here.

"Mr. Miller." The voice carried again, this time sounding closer.

"Come along, sir." The sailor nudged him in the side.

"Someone is calling me."

"Miller's a common name. No more delays."

Mark took another step toward the train.

"Mr. Miller, stop. I insist." Mark turned and saw Desch huffing toward him. "Good night, man, making me run like that." Desch took an envelope from his coat pocket and handed it to one of the MPs. "This informs you that Mr. Miller is to come with me. Signed by Admiral Meader himself." Desch winked at Mark. "There are limited advantages to having the man live with me. One is obtaining a get-out-of-the-service letter on a weekend. Come along."

"We can't let you take him."

"You will. And if there are any problems, you'll find him at NCR working for me. Good day, gentlemen."

The MP opened the letter and read it as they walked away. "Thank you, sir."

"Next time let me know so I don't have to pull you from the train itself."

"Yes, sir."

"You've got a young woman to thank for letting me know your predicament. Ensign Happ determined you shouldn't take that train, and I agree with her."

Evelyn?

"Come along. Back to work with you. There's much to be done."

ten

"Join us for the company ball game?"

Evelyn looked up to find Mark standing over her, a gleam in his eyes. "I don't know. I'm not much into sports."

"Come now. I don't buy that for a moment. As competitive as you are in here, I imagine you're a killer on the field."

Was that a compliment? And did it mean he saw her as one of the guys rather than as a woman? The thought caused her stomach to sink. "I'd hate to kill your impression of me."

He studied her a moment. "I don't think you could do that."

Somehow, when he looked at her, she wanted him to see her as a woman, not as another one of the guys working to solve an engineering problem. The more time she spent with him, the more important that became. There were too few men like him. Intelligent. Kind. Genuine. Handsome. Her thoughts pulled her up short. After so much time wanting to join the engineering group, now she found that wasn't the end of what she wanted after all. No, she needed Mark to see her as a woman.

"Earth to Evelyn." He tapped her gently on the side of her head, then toyed with one of her curls. The look in his eyes softened, and he let go of her hair like it had branded him. "Well, I hope you join us." He backed away from her as if a platoon of Germans prepared to attack.

❧

What just happened? A friendly conversation had somehow taken a deeper turn, and Mark felt like he had waded in the deep waters of the Miami River in flood stage.

John walked into the room, then did a double take. "Seen a ghost, Miller?"

"Look that good, huh?"

"Actually, more like you need a chair. What happened?"

Other than touching hair that felt softer than down? Reading a pair of eyes that said so much more than Evelyn probably knew. "Nothing. Guess I'll take a break."

"It's marginally cooler outside than it is in here with that beast. Never thought I'd complain about it running more consistently."

Mark nodded. "Let's get the other fifteen running well; then we'll see what heat is." He hurried from the room. Paige. He needed to spend some time with her. That would undo whatever had just happened with Evelyn. He called Paige's image to mind. She was about as opposite of Evelyn as one could get. Where Paige was blond and willowy, Evelyn was dark and curvaceous. Where Paige worked with children and seemed inclined to motherhood, Evelyn challenged his mind and had never given an indication she dreamed of a family. Where Paige delighted in frills and feminine wiles, Evelyn lived in uniform. One loved the Lord, and the other didn't. That last factor ended the comparison.

He walked across the tracks to the rest of the NCR complex. *Father, I don't know what happened.* That wasn't entirely true. He'd suddenly seen Evelyn as more than another intelligent mind. She was more, much more. *Okay, You see the trouble here. Help me focus on the things that matter to You.*

If his thoughts wandered like this with one touch of the softest curls he'd ever felt, was Paige the woman for him?

The question left him groaning. What a weak person.

And he thought he was strong? No, he was a fool.

❧

Saturday, Mark picked Paige up on his way to Sugar Camp. The company had decided to take the action to the WAVES, and Mark knew he needed Paige at his side to remind him why Evelyn couldn't be anything more than a friend. Albeit an attractive friend. Paige bubbled over with anecdotes from helping in the children's section at the library.

"You should see the adorable children. I could eat them up."

"I'm glad you enjoy it."

"Adore it." She touched his arm with a light, yet electric touch. "Are you okay? You're distant."

"Another long week." He shrugged. "Almost getting shipped off Monday set the tone."

"I'm so glad that didn't happen."

"Would you have missed me?" He needed to know. Was he merely a pleasant diversion? Or more?

"What a question." He caught her studying him. "You know how I feel about you. You're the only man I spend time with, the only one I want to. What more do you want from our relationship?"

That was the million-dollar question. Silence settled over the car as he turned into Sugar Camp.

"Your silence says it all, Mark." She flounced around in the seat. He parked the car then turned to Paige. He stroked her cheek, and she leaned into his caress. "I'm sorry, Paige. It's a question I need to answer after praying some more." He got out and rounded the car to open her door. "Thanks for coming with me today. I wanted to spend the time with you."

She nodded, a ghost of a smile shadowing her face as she accepted his help.

Mark grabbed the blanket and picnic basket his mom had packed from the car's boot. "Shall we?"

They strolled across the lawn toward the recreation area.

"Miller. About time you showed up. We were ready to start the game without you." John yelled across the ball diamond while slapping his glove against his thigh.

"Will you be okay?" Mark situated the blanket on the ground, placing the basket on top.

Paige nodded. "Of course. Go play. I'll cheer from here."

He watched her settle on the blanket, skirt splayed around her like the petals of a vibrant flower. She blew him a kiss.

He grabbed his mitt from the basket, then jogged to the diamond. "Needed me to win?"

John guffawed. "That's right. We needed the all-powerful Miller to ensure success."

The other men laughed.

Mark jogged to the outfield and pulled his cap lower to shade his eyes. This was what he needed. Fresh air. A beautiful woman. And the chance to take out his frustration on a small ball.

&

Cheers carried on the sultry breeze. The cabin that had felt like a freezer when Evelyn had arrived in May now felt like an oven. Since eleven o'clock, cars had pulled into Sugar Camp bringing an equal contingent of sailors and civilians to her hideaway. Mark Miller worked his magic somewhere in that mix.

Evelyn didn't think of herself as a coward, but still she hid in the cabin. Evelyn Happ. Hiding from a man. Something she'd never done before. But one careless touch had never shifted the foundations of her world.

She didn't want to like Mark.

To him she was another brain. At one time, that had been everything she'd wanted, to be accepted like one of the guys.

Now that wasn't good enough.

And that hand touching her curls, a simple touch, indicated he might if he let himself.

If that was true, why sweat alone in her cabin? She could enjoy the day's events with everyone else. Sweat dripped down her back, punctuating her foolishness. Evelyn grabbed her hairbrush and pulled it through her curls, fighting the tangles. She applied lipstick and ran out the door. The air outside the cabin felt marginally warmer, but at least a breeze stirred the trees.

She hurried to the baseball diamond.

"There you are." Vivian looked up from a blanket where she sat with several sailors. "I wondered if I'd get to entertain these fine men all by myself."

"That would be such a hardship." Evelyn sank to the

blanket and smiled at the sailors.

Viv considered the group. "You have a point. Gentlemen, my roommate Evelyn Happ. Don't let her appearance deceive you. She's a brain."

"Thanks, I think." Evelyn shook her head. She settled her legs underneath her, and soon, the conversation volleyed among them as she learned about the sailors. She kept half her attention on the field, keeping tabs on Mark. He played some position out in the field far away from the action. An ensign hit a ball so hard the bat shattered. Mark jigged around the field as he worked his way under the ball. Evelyn cheered when he caught the ball and held it up in his glove.

"Out!" shouted the umpire.

Mark's team cheered, so it must have been an important play.

"You still with us?" Viv teased.

"Hmm. Enjoying a moment of the game."

Viv leaned close to her and whispered. "The game or the player?" She winked at Evelyn, and heat flamed Evelyn's cheeks.

"Never mind." She turned to one of the sailors and began to pull his story from him. Anything to get the focus off her.

෴

Mark joined Paige on her blanket when he got relieved during the next inning. "What did you think?"

"Other than that you were a heroic player?"

Her word choice made him chuckle. "I don't know about heroic."

"You made the winning play." She raised her eyebrows and stared at him from under the rim of her hat.

"Not exactly the winning play, but it ended the inning."

"See. That's my point." She smiled, admiration filling her face. "You were the hero."

He leaned back on his elbows, uncomfortable with the adoration that filled her gaze. Mark watched the game for a minute and decided the guys were doing fine without him. As

A Promise Born 85

two men rounded the bases toward home, he pointed Paige toward them. "See, the team's performing better without me."

"A fluke. That's all. If you were in, they'd score three runs." She pulled a container out of the basket and set it in front of him. "Your mother prepared a feast for us."

"She expects me to feed half the team."

"Really? Well, I want to keep you to myself, young man." She swept her arm around to take in the crowd. "Even if I share with a crowd."

He followed her motion until his gaze landed on the party at a blanket a hundred feet from his. Evelyn sat on it with another WAVES and what looked to be six or seven sailors. The enlisted men were each in positions that made it clear they wanted Evelyn's undivided attention. She didn't appear to favor any one over another, but he suddenly wanted to leave Paige and walk over there and chase the others away. Evelyn needed someone to keep away the riffraff. He started to get up, when a hand touched his sleeve.

"Mark?"

He startled and turned back to Paige. "Yes?"

She smiled, but it looked brittle. "Nothing." She pulled out a packet of cookies. "Here you go."

Mark settled back on the blanket and accepted a peanut butter cookie before eating it in two bites. Paige wrinkled her nose at his manners, but he didn't care. Instead, he wondered why, sitting here with a beautiful woman, he kept thinking of one a hundred yards away whom he could never have.

Paige turned back to the basket, and he sneaked a peek in Evelyn's direction. She laughed at something, the faint sound reaching him.

"You coming back in, Miller?" John stood at the edge of the diamond, glove on hip, staring at Mark.

"Think you need me?"

"I don't know that we'll ever *need* you, but if you'd like to join in, we've got a spot."

Paige pouted when he stood and brushed his pants off.

"That wasn't long enough."

"You heard John. Duty calls."

"It always does. And this is only a ballgame." She crossed her arms and looked away. Her jaw tightened, then she considered him a moment. "All right. I'm sorry. Enjoy your chance to play."

"I'll be back after this inning." Mark stood, and his gaze collided with Evelyn's. Her smile jolted him to his core.

eleven

Unable to fight back a yawn, Evelyn stretched and noticed the hands of the clock had crept to eight o'clock. Her shift had long since ended, but the work hadn't. So Evelyn found herself listening to Adam race through another run. She must look like a wilted flower after twelve hours monitoring the machine.

"That's all for now, gentlemen." Desch looked around at the few hardy souls. He caught himself when he saw Evelyn. "And Ensign Happ. We'll try again tomorrow."

"Yes, sir." Evelyn tried to shrug off the sting of being lumped in with the men. As the only woman engineer, it happened often, a regular occupational hazard. But at times like this, she wished she wasn't such an afterthought.

Since Mr. Desch had called it quits in the middle of a shift, she couldn't join other WAVES for the walk back to Sugar Camp. She didn't relish the idea of walking home alone, even though this early in July, the sky was still light. Then her stomach grumbled its protest that she hadn't fed it since noon. The thought of eating another cafeteria meal had her swallowing against bile.

She surveyed Adam. The original two machines had multiplied to four and now sixteen. The number made a small dent in the production the navy demanded. The only problem was none of the machines worked consistently.

Mark insisted they'd find a solution. Even quoted the Bible to support that idea, but Evelyn couldn't join him in his confidence. And she'd seen the fatigue and despair that teased him.

She shook her head to clear the thought. The Bombes were the last thing she wanted to think about. She needed at least a few hours' break. As for Mark, she didn't know what to think about him. Her thoughts returned to him too often—especially for a man who chose to ignore the potential fire that flashed between them in unguarded moments.

The door opened and closed, causing Evelyn to look around the room. If she didn't hurry, she'd be left alone. She pinned her hat in place and slid on her suit jacket.

Mark already had his hat and briefcase and stood by the office door.

"Thanks for waiting, Mark." Often he was the only man who lingered or exercised the common courtesies.

"Join me for dinner?" Mark stepped back as if stunned by what he'd said.

She waited to see if he'd revoke the offer. Suddenly, she wanted nothing more than time alone with him.

"In the cafeteria?" Must have decided to stick with his words.

"I'd love to join you, but not the cafeteria. We'll have to eat there tomorrow." She took his arm. "Right now, we're free, so let's find a restaurant."

"One open now?"

"Even if it's pie and coffee. Please?"

"All right. I know the place."

For an unexplainable reason she felt taller as she walked beside him. It felt so right to be on his arm headed to dinner. "Where are you taking me?"

"It's a surprise. And if we're lucky, we'll catch the trolley downtown."

Mark picked up his pace as they walked down the sidewalk toward the trolley stop. Evelyn double-timed to keep up. No matter how she tried to tease their destination from him, he refused to give it. Maybe the mischievous boy his mother had told her about still existed under all the education and responsibility. A trolley pulled up at the stop. Mark helped her board, deposited coins for their fare, and guided her to a seat. The trolley generated a breeze that felt wonderful. Evelyn considered taking off her hat and letting the breeze ruffle her curls but stopped short when she caught Mark watching her. That annoying heat warmed her neck and cheeks. She could only hope in the fading light he attributed it to the summer heat rather than to his attention.

Mark rolled his neck, waves of fatigue and tension rolling off him. "I'll be glad when this project is over."

"Really?" Evelyn stared at him, trying to fathom feeling that way. "This project is one of the best things that ever happened to me."

The trolley pulled to the curb for the Union Station stop. Mark pulled her to her feet and stepped back to avoid bumping against her.

"Even the long hours? It's a job, Evelyn. There will be others after the war, and maybe those will allow us to work more regular shifts." Mark led her down the sidewalk in front of the station.

"I disagree. This project has allowed me to do something I've never done before."

"What? Contribute? There's more to you than your mind." He glanced at her. "Much more."

If he believed that, why did he continue to hold her at arm's length, never allowing her access beyond a certain point? She'd thought she understood men, but if Mark's behavior served as a proxy for men, she was sorely mistaken.

He led the way to a hole-in-the-wall restaurant that she would have missed in a casual walk-by. "It doesn't look like much, but they serve Mehaffie's pies here. Incredible. Melt in your mouth."

When he opened the door, Evelyn scanned the interior. A single lit candle dotted each bistro table's blue-checkered cloth. A warm, fruity smell caused her stomach to grumble.

Mark grinned as Evelyn pushed a hand against her stomach. "I take it this will work for you."

"I think so." A vacant table by the window beckoned her. "Can we sit there? I'd love to watch whoever is walking by outside."

"Sure." Mark helped her with her chair and settled on the opposite side of the table. "What would you like to try? I'll get it from the counter."

"Counter? I didn't notice it."

"During busier hours, someone comes to your table. But after eight, Antonio makes the patrons do the work."

Evelyn looked around the empty dining room. "That explains the lack of clientele. I'll take a slice of whatever pie you recommend and a cup of coffee."

A few moments later, Mark returned with a precariously balanced stack of two plates with pie slices and two mugs. Evelyn giggled as he bowed his head, announcing, "Your order, mademoiselle. A slice of Dutch apple or Boston cream along with a mug of perfectly doctored tea. They're out of coffee."

"The apple, please." She grabbed the mug from its precarious position and took a sip. The symphony of flavors hit the perfect note. "How did you know how I like it?"

"Let's see. I've worked with you for more than a month and you regularly drink the stuff with my mom. Plenty of time to notice you prefer milk and whatever sweet is available."

Evelyn stared into the mug. What kind of man noticed those details? A man who could work his way into her heart without much effort. She took a bite of the pie, enjoying the blend of apple, cinnamon, and crumb topping. "Much better than the cafeteria."

As they talked about families and childhood, Evelyn realized this was the first time she'd been alone with Mark. Every other time, they'd been chaperoned by his family, colleagues, or a crowd. The Mark she saw now was every bit as wonderful as she'd imagined. Self-deprecating charm mixed with self-assurance. The man knew who he was. Something about his quiet confidence and inner strength called to her.

Their empty plates had sat on the table for a while when Mark glanced at his watch. He shifted in his seat and smiled ruefully. "I need to get you home."

"Yes. We'll have to be back at NCR all too soon." Evelyn grabbed her purse from the corner of the table. Mark hailed a cab and directed the driver to take them to Sugar Camp. After they arrived, he released the cab and walked her to the main gate, Evelyn feeling the spark each time they bumped into each other. "Thank you. For tonight."

"I enjoyed it, too."

Evelyn hesitated, unsure whether to leave him at the gate or wait. She took a step down the path.

"Wait." Mark's voice beckoned her back.

"Yes?"

He chucked under her chin, and she fought the desire to lean into his touch. Turn it into a caress.

"Evelyn, you are an amazing woman." The shadows couldn't hide the intensity in his gaze. Slowly, he leaned down. Time stilled. When the barest distance separated them, he stopped. Evelyn closed her eyes, breath hitched as she anticipated the connection. He exhaled a breath, and she sensed him pull back. "See you in the morning." His lips brushed her cheek.

She opened her eyes and watched him go, an unsettled sensation cloaking her. She shouldn't have wanted his kiss as much as she had. Not when he belonged to another girl—at least as far as she knew. She closed her eyes against the knowledge. Maybe Mark was no different from the other men out there. Especially the ones she'd entrusted her heart to in the past. The ones willing to kiss any girl who presented herself. Maybe she wasn't so special, after all. How could she be when another woman stood center stage? With a heavy feeling in her stomach, she turned and walked to her cabin.

❧

Walking in darkness was the perfect punishment for a man like him. Mark couldn't believe what had happened at Sugar Camp. He refused to look back, even though every fiber of his being wanted to know if Evelyn stormed away or waited.

What had he done?

Though he may have stopped short of kissing her lips, he'd left her with little doubt of where his thoughts lay. This was a relationship he couldn't pursue. And if his actions somehow became an obstacle to her finding Christ. . .

God, forgive me.

The words seemed so insufficient.

And what about Paige? What had he done? He was a fool. The truth in stark terms.

He knew better. The Bible was clear. Do not be unequally yoked. That had to apply to all stages of a relationship or it had no meaning at all. He tore his hat off, slapped it against his thigh, and shoved it back on his head.

When he reached home, he hoped he'd escape notice and slip away to his room. But a light in the living room beckoned him. His father sat in his chair, paper in hand.

"Welcome home, son."

"Father." Mark sank into the matching chair on the other side of the fireplace.

Father eyed him over the top of the paper before folding it and setting it to the side. "What's bothering you?"

Mark searched for words. How to explain without his father becoming disgusted with him? "How did you know Mother was the woman you wanted to spend the rest of your life with?"

A wry chuckle erupted from Father. "Does this mean you think Paige is the woman for you?"

"Yes. . .no. . .maybe. . .I don't know." Mark ran his fingers through his hair. "It's complicated."

"Must be. Probably by a certain woman we've come to know."

"Maybe." Mark groaned. "But there's a problem."

"A pretty big one."

"I should focus on Paige, but something is missing."

"Love is more than fireworks, son."

"But shouldn't that be part of it? Shouldn't there be an

element of feeling like this woman is the most amazing person in the world and you want to be worthy of her affection?"

Father leaned forward, elbows on his knees. "But if she doesn't share your faith. . ."

"I know." Mark stood and paced with his hands in his pockets as he worked to moderate his voice. "I can't forget that fact no matter how I try. This woman who challenges me and intrigues me doesn't share the most important thing in my life. And I don't know what to do about it."

"I can speak to your mother about not inviting Miss Happ over for Sunday lunches anymore."

"No." Mark shook his head. "I wouldn't rob her of the friendship. She enjoys it too much."

"Your mother?"

"Evelyn."

"What happened tonight?"

"Why?"

"You don't get this upset unless something specific has happened."

Mark blinked, wishing he had a means of escape, but honesty required nothing less than the truth. "Evelyn and I went to dinner tonight after we got off. It had been a long, frustrating day. I asked her to join me, and she agreed." Mark sighed. "I walked her home."

"And something more happened." Father patted the chair. "Sit down, son. Let's pray. You're a man and must make your own decisions, but let's bathe those in prayer first."

Mark settled down next to him and listened to the words that washed over him on the way to heaven's throne room. God's grace would cover him. But what would Evelyn do?

twelve

The morning following her dining catastrophe with Mark, Evelyn seriously considered missing work. Surely a confused and battered heart qualified as sickness. The thought of facing Mark and trying to work with him exhausted her.

Evelyn didn't think she could pretend nothing had happened, even though technically nothing had. Mark hadn't kissed her.

No, he'd just lowered his head within a millimeter of her lips, then retreated to her cheek.

Who was she fooling?

The only reason a man like Mark retreated was if she didn't match his criteria in some way. Or because he still cared for Paige. But how could he after last night? After hours tossing and turning, Evelyn remained unsettled. She needed to ask Mark some tough questions, the kind she'd rather ignore. But her heart wouldn't let her. No, she needed the truth. Did she fail his unspoken criteria, or did he love Paige and had he merely toyed with her? The possible answers scared her, but she had to know.

"Evelyn Happ, snap awake." Vivian stood in front of her bunk and pulled the covers back. "Get up. The government doesn't care why you're moping."

Lonnie walked out of the bathroom. "Next."

"You're right." Somehow she'd face the man. At least machines acted in a rational manner. "Don't worry about me, Viv. I'll be fine."

Viv didn't look convinced. "That settles it. I'm arranging a weekend filled with fun, activities, and dates. You need to get away from Mark Miller for a while."

"Fine." Evelyn didn't have time to focus Viv on something

else. She'd go along this weekend. "But right now, I need to fly."

Evelyn hurried through her morning routine and raced to the marching area, arriving in time to join the formation. A moment later, they started the march down the hill to NCR. When a man headed in the opposite direction pulled over and offered a ride to any WAVES who wanted one, Evelyn was sorely tempted. Instead, she kept her eyes locked forward.

If only she could do that the balance of the day and avoid any run-ins with Mark. Then the day would be a success.

❧

Meader marched into Adam's room, a magazine under his arm. Mark braced for the daily barrage of reasons the project wasn't moving fast enough as Meader slapped the most recent issue of *Life* on the table. Mark winced when he saw the cover. Several soldiers carried a casket draped with an American flag. He knew from reading his mom's copy that the inside contained a list of American dead in the war. He didn't want to think how the list would grow between the early July issue and the end of hostilities.

"Gentlemen, this is precisely why your efforts are not good enough." Meader jabbed a finger on the photo of the coffin. His face was red as he strode to tower over a seated Desch. "You must get the machines working. Now! Any more delays and our efforts will be pulled by Washington. We are out of time." He looked at each person in the room, then spun on his heel and left, leaving the magazine on the table.

Desch picked it up and tossed it to the side. "You heard the man. Back to work."

The words fell heavy in the room.

Evelyn fingered the magazine's pages, cheeks washed of color. "We've considered which parts are most likely to break down under the strain of the speeds you demand. Did we miss any?"

"Of course not." John's voice carried the frustration of

months of fruitless efforts.

"Ensign Happ is correct." Desch pulled off his glasses and pinched his nose. "We need to look at this from a different angle. Let's break the machine into the basic pieces critical to its function."

As they had many times before, the engineers itemized the pieces while Evelyn took notes. They broke into small groups to consider how the pieces might factor into the breakdowns. Evelyn practically ran across the room to join the group farthest from Mark's.

Hours later, Desch called them back to his table. A tight smile etched his face. Desch held a rotor and eased sandpaper over it and back. "You see, gentlemen. Sometimes we forget the practical solutions in our focus for theoretical applications and success." Desch pulled a brush from his back pocket and swept it lightly over the surface. "Let's try this."

Mark wanted to believe this would fix the ongoing problem. But could the multiple problems with the Bombes come down to something as simple as slightly uneven rotor surfaces? If it worked, Desch would be a hero.

Desch handed him a rotor. "Get to work, Mr. Miller. You sand while we watch the machine."

"Yes, sir."

"Mr. Fields, here's one for you, too."

John reluctantly accepted the items. "I'll break the rotors."

"That's why when this works, we'll give the sanding to the women with their delicate fingers and control." He smiled at Evelyn. "But for today, I want you to experience what's needed to make these rotors work. Get to it. Gently now."

Mark sanded his rotor cautiously. Desch's theory made sense. At the speeds the machines worked, even tiny variations on the surface of the rotors could cause anomalies.

Evelyn huddled on the other side of the group, chewing on a fingernail, something she only did when stressed or upset. Had he caused that, or did it stem from the pressure Meader had dumped on the room? Her rush to avoid him prevented him from apologizing or fixing the mess he'd made.

All day, he'd been plagued by a simple question. It echoed in the recesses of his mind. *What would Jesus do?* The lingering question stemmed from the book he'd recently finished, Charles Sheldon's *In His Steps*. There was no question Christ hadn't been honored by his actions last night. But He could be honored by how Mark chose to behave from here on out.

That was the rub.

He knew no way to apologize and right his wrong other than to force Evelyn to talk to him. How could that be Christ honoring? He must proceed cautiously. Especially when Evelyn didn't share his faith. How could he make her understand without coming across as haughty?

And then there was his relationship with Paige. He must resolve how he felt about her. It wasn't fair to waver, especially when a woman like Evelyn could make him forget Paige. He certainly hadn't honored her last night.

So he took the easy road, the coward's path. He worked as hard to avoid her as she did to avoid him.

❧

Even though Mr. Desch had given Evelyn permission to leave at the end of her shift with the rest of the WAVES, she felt like a coward as she snuck from Adam's room. Part of her didn't care as long as she avoided finding herself alone with Mark again. Not that he'd given any indication he'd seek her out. No, he seemed as inclined as she to ignore the whole mess between them. The thought of a repeat of last night's stolen moments and kiss caused her stomach to flip.

She hurried to join Lonnie as the WAVES prepared for the walk back to Sugar Camp.

The redhead looked at her, concern pinching her face. "Are you okay? You look pale."

Better not to explain. Lonnie'd tell Viv, and Viv would hunt for someone to distract Evelyn. The woman had already promised to distract her. Viv certainly didn't need the encouragement. Another man wasn't what Evelyn needed. At all.

"Guess I'm tired."

"After your late night, I'm not surprised. When did you sneak into the cabin?"

The WAVES swung into action, marching four abreast out of the building and onto the street.

"Late." Far too late for her battered heart. How would she feel if Mark had actually finished the kiss? Evelyn didn't want to know and didn't want Lonnie probing. She quickly brought up the article about leg makeup in *Life*. Before long, Lonnie launched into a monologue about a USO event she'd attended. Not what Evelyn had in mind when she brought up the topic, but much better than her futile, confused thoughts.

The early days of July ticked by in the routine monotony of work. The Fourth of July fell on a Sunday, so the afternoon was filled with a picnic, speeches, and then fireworks as the night sky darkened. It created a welcome break from the pressure of Washington's deadlines. Evelyn longed for pockets of time to relax and break the monotony. Finally one Wednesday, her shift of WAVES along with the rest of Building 26 was dismissed early to attend a ceremony at Sugar Camp. A ripple of excitement pulsed through Evelyn. This was something different.

She needed a few moments to freshen up with the girls in the cabin before heading to the parade grounds. Chairs for the visitors and VIPs had appeared while she worked. The WAVES and a large contingent of sailors and officers from Patterson would congregate on one side of the field as they prepared to parade past guests and dignitaries. Then they'd clamor for seats, too.

Lonnie straightened her white summer cap against her red hair. Her freckles had popped out in greater numbers since the gals had started using the camp pool. "Do you think all that marching we did in basic training will pay off?"

"Sure. Remember to keep going no matter what happens or who passes out." Viv sat on Evelyn's bed, scrubbing her white shoes. "How do they expect us to keep these silly things clean enough for inspection?" She tossed the cloth to the side. "We're not stopping, right? Just marching across the field?"

Evelyn nodded. "That's what the lieutenant indicated."

Lonnie groaned. "I hope we don't look out of practice. Imagine the brass getting us up in the morning to march."

"More than to get to Building 26 and back?" Evelyn wrinkled her nose at the thought.

"We'll be brilliant." Viv hooked arms with the other two and pulled them out of the cabin and across the parade grounds. "Have you seen all the servicemen here? Some are from Patterson." Her words tumbled over each other. The gal never slowed down in her hunt.

They reached the formation point, and Evelyn wondered which of the seamen in their summer whites was the radioman who would receive the Purple Heart.

Lonnie looked the crowd over. "You know, I think the only reason they're doing the ceremony here is to get more war bonds out of NCR."

"You are incredibly cynical, Lonnie."

The woman shrugged. "Maybe, but watch, they'll turn this into a publicity event." She took a breath and lowered her voice. "This sailor has done his part; now you do yours."

A large group of civilians attended the event. Some Evelyn recognized from NCR. Then she saw Mark. Things remained awkward between them, and she didn't know how to change that. She wanted to ask him outright why he had tried to kiss her. Ask about Paige. But both topics could lead to uncomfortable questions about why she cared. Questions she'd rather avoid.

Evelyn marched in step with the other WAVES past the officers and civilian bigwigs. Even as she marched, she had a heightened awareness of where Mark stood.

The review ended, and Admiral Meader took the stage to present the Purple Heart. The WAVES joined the crowd,

Evelyn hunting for a piece of shade others hadn't already claimed.

Lonnie leaned toward Evelyn. "Meader's droning."

Evelyn agreed. "It's still exciting to think this man is receiving the Purple Heart."

"I suppose." Lonnie kept her eyes fixed ahead, but Evelyn could tell she'd stopped listening.

When the ceremony ended, Evelyn waited for the crowd to disperse. No need to push her way through it back to a sweltering cabin. As she lingered, she wondered if Mark would make any effort to approach her. Maybe things would feel different since they weren't in the stilted work environment.

She shaded her eyes with her hand and stood on tiptoe, searching the crowd for him. A lump filled her throat when she spied him watching her, shoulders slumped and eyes heavy.

❧

Evelyn's gaze hit Mark with the force of a Sherman tank.

He needed Paige with him, a very visible reminder of why Evelyn could not be the woman for him. Because when he looked at Evelyn, saw the pain filling her eyes, Mark fought to walk away.

If he walked home, he'd pass by Evelyn. He sucked in a breath, then started that way. His mother's words cycled through his head. He needed to settle down. Find a woman who would love him completely. A woman who understood him.

Whenever she talked like that, he got the distinct impression she didn't have Paige in mind.

John waltzed up to him and bumped his shoulder. "Can you believe we got the afternoon off? My wife will be thrilled to see me before dark."

"You'd better get moving." Mark looked at his watch. "It's already four o'clock."

"Don't you have somewhere to enjoy the break?" John grinned. "A date with your girl? Round up a baseball game?"

"I don't know. I've got something I have to do first." Mark squared his jaw and set his shoulders. He needed to confront the problem with Evelyn head-on.

John scanned the crowd, yet seemed to understand Mark meant Evelyn. "Good luck with that, buddy. She's a hard woman to read."

Truer words had never been spoken.

"But you need to get her back on the team. She's been out of it the last week. It'd better not be because of you." John clapped him on the back. "See you tomorrow."

Mark watched him go and found Evelyn again. Her stance challenged him not to back down, hinting she fully expected him to turn and leave. Again.

A few more steps, and he stood in front of her. "Hello, Evelyn."

"Mark." Her tone wasn't cold but missed its usual warmth.

"Do you have plans right now?"

She studied him a moment. "I don't know. Is that an invitation?"

He shoved his hands in his pockets. "Yes. We need to clear the air before it affects our work."

Her eyes hardened. "Can I risk going somewhere with you?"

Ouch. He'd earned that. "Just for a moment. We can stay somewhere very public." And with the sun shining, they'd avoid duplicating the night's dark cloak of intimacy.

She seemed to weigh something in her mind before nodding. "All right. But only for a few minutes."

He tucked her hand on his arm, pausing when a jolt shook him at her light touch. He could not allow himself to go there. She was wrong for him, and surely he had to be for her, too. A fool. He was one if he thought they could find a way to make a relationship work.

"You wanted something?" Evelyn's soft voice pulled him from his thoughts.

"I wanted to apologize. For the other night."

"Which night?" So she wouldn't be easy on him.

"The night we went to the café after work." Her look dared him to admit it. "When I almost kissed you."

"Don't say it." Evelyn tugged away from his arm.

"What?"

"That you're sorry. That it was a mistake. That it never should have happened."

"But it's true."

She shook her head. "No, there's more to us than that."

"There is no us, Evelyn." He ran his hands through his hair and paced in front of her. "I shouldn't have kissed you."

"You didn't." A storm gathered on her face.

"I wanted to."

"And I wanted you to."

"That's precisely why I couldn't." The thought of fighting Evelyn pained him. He stopped, turned to her, and placed his hands on her arms. She tensed as if prepared to run.

❧

Evelyn froze. Dared she take this conversation deeper, or should she leave? She couldn't walk away, not if she wanted to understand what had happened. Suddenly, all she wanted was to force Mark to explain himself and his actions. "I thought you cared for me." She locked her gaze with his and refused to give him quarter.

"I do. But we must act on more than emotion, Evelyn. Much more." Mark sighed, then heaved in a breath.

Evelyn stared at him. "Why? Because of Paige? Do you feel for her what you feel for me?" She bit her lower lip as she waited for his answer.

The color drained from his face, but Mark didn't speak.

"You can't say it, can you? Can't admit your feelings for her. Do you have any?" People turned to stare, and Evelyn fought to keep her voice low. "Or are you no better than other men? Willing to take whatever you can from women. And if that means playing with two, so be it." She choked on the words. "I thought you were different. Better than that. Guess I was wrong."

"Wait a minute. That's not fair."

"It isn't? Then tell me you're no longer dating Paige."

"I can't." He rubbed his hair. "I wish I could sort this out. It's complicated."

"What's so complicated about acknowledging what we have? Why don't your feelings, my feelings, matter?" She held up her hand, blocking the words before he could speak. "Don't tell me something insincere. I deserve the truth. All of it." She wanted to stamp her foot like a petulant child.

Pain filled Mark's eyes. "It doesn't matter what I want."

"That is absurd. Has Paige placed you under a spell? Removed your free will?"

"No. It's not like that."

"What is it? What does she have that I don't?"

Mark's face tightened, and his eyes looked into the distance. Evelyn wanted to hold his face and force him to look at her. Force him to see her.

"You wouldn't understand my reasons."

"Do not decide for me what I can handle. All I want is honesty. If you're going to steal a kiss, you'd better explain why I'm not good enough for you." Tears pricked her eyes, and she batted against them. "I deserve that."

"You don't believe."

What? That was why he didn't want her? She stepped back under the weight of those three words. "Faith? Faith is more important to you than this?" She gestured between them. "That's your excuse." A sob escaped, and she clamped a hand over her mouth. He took a step toward her, but she took another step back and held up her hand, blocking him. "Stay away."

"Evelyn. . ." Mark reached for her.

"No, stay away." She turned and fled.

thirteen

For most of the evening, the activity in the cafeteria and cabin distracted Evelyn from her downward-spiraling thoughts. She tried flipping through *Life* and other magazines, but none of the stories held her attention. Even the images from the war couldn't silence Mark's words. Tears battled her anger, until both raged through her.

With nothing else working, Evelyn picked up the Bible Mrs. Miller had loaned her and flipped to her bookmark. Genesis seemed a fanciful tale, but the Jesus portrayed in John—she didn't know what to think about Him. The words might be English, but the meaning seemed deeper, difficult to uncover. *"I am the vine, ye are the branches."* What did that mean? She tossed the book back on the table.

Mary Ellen was the last woman to make it back to the cabin. She held a book under her arm, and peace radiated from her.

"Where have you been?" Evelyn snapped, then shrugged. "Sorry."

"One of the gals in my room at work invited me to a meeting." Mary Ellen shrugged. "It's a book club of sorts."

Viv bounced next to Evelyn on the bunk, hair pulled back and pajamas on. "What are you reading? Maybe I'll join you next time."

"I don't know that it would interest you." She held out the book. Evelyn saw it was the Bible. "We're reading the book of John." She caressed the cover. "I've attended church all my life, but I've never explored it this way. You should have heard the women discussing each verse. They didn't agree all the time, but they respected each other and the book."

Mary Ellen's description intrigued Evelyn. Maybe this was

what she needed. And she wanted to understand what Mary Ellen seemed to have found at the meeting. "Could I come?"

"I'd like that." Mary Ellen slipped the book under her pillow, then smiled shyly before heading into the bathroom.

"I knew you were upset, but this?" Viv looked at Evelyn like she'd just suggested joining a convent. "We have got to work you out of this mood."

Viv climbed onto her top bunk, while Evelyn lay down. She put her hands behind her head and studied the underside of Viv's bunk. Prior to arriving in Dayton, she hadn't thought about faith. Life was something to live to the fullest while you could. But if faith mattered to Mary Ellen and the Millers, she needed to explore it more. Not because of Mark's painful words.

No, gaining Mark's approval was the wrong reason to search.

If she participated, it must be for the right reasons. And this book club would give her a way to search without spending Sunday mornings with Mark. She'd miss spending time with Mrs. Miller, but she needed distance from Mark. Working with him was painful enough. No need to force herself to spend her free day watching him and hearing his words over and over again.

The next week, Evelyn walked across the Sugar Camp campus with Mary Ellen. The woman allowed silence to settle between them, and Evelyn didn't feel like carrying a conversation. Part of her wanted to run back to the cabin or anywhere else. Why had she thought joining the meeting a good idea?

Every reason abandoned her. Along with her good sense, it appeared.

Mary Ellen led the way to a corner of the cafeteria. "We meet here, then head to the amphitheater or another spot that's open."

Evelyn nodded and followed her to an area where about twenty women had gathered. Not all of the women were

WAVES, which surprised her. Then she saw Marjorie Miller. Evelyn turned to leave; she'd explain to Mary Ellen later. She couldn't face Marjorie right now. Not with things so awkward with Mark. She'd avoided going to church and having lunch with the Millers by pleading the need to catch up on her sleep.

"Evelyn." The quiet voice stopped her. She turned to find Marjorie standing behind her, a light in her eyes. So much for escaping. "I'm so delighted you're joining us. Did you come with Mary Ellen?"

"Yes, ma'am. She looked so. . .happy after last week's meeting I had to come see what it's about."

"Mary Ellen did seem like a sponge." Marjorie laughed before studying Evelyn. "You aren't avoiding us, are you?"

"Um, avoiding you?" Evelyn felt a pang of guilt.

"Yes." Marjorie led her to a table a few feet away from the others. "Has something happened between you and Mark?"

Evelyn grimaced. She didn't want to have this conversation. Not now. Not with Marjorie.

"Call it a mother's intuition, but when you haven't joined us on Sundays, and Mark's lived in his own world, I wonder."

"You needn't worry. Mark has his girl, and I'm only here awhile." Evelyn's fingers fidgeted with the tablecloth, twisting it into rosettes and releasing.

Marjorie leaned forward and placed her hand on top of Evelyn's. She opened her mouth, as if to say something, but stopped when a woman called the group to order. She squeezed Evelyn's hand. "We'll talk later."

Tears warred with the thought of running far from this kind woman who genuinely cared. Evelyn's friendship with the Millers had been a highlight of her time in Dayton, but now it felt as awkward as her interactions with Mark. She took a deep breath. She couldn't leave now without disrupting everything, so she settled in. The women sang a song, one unfamiliar to Evelyn. The lyrics settled over her, the women's voices mingling in sweet harmony. After the last note, the leader opened the Bible in front of her on the table. Each of the other women had a matching book. Evelyn felt like sliding under the table. She should have grabbed the one Marjorie had lent her. Marjorie brought her chair around and slid her Bible between them. She pointed to the woman at the front. "Our leader tonight is Patricia Hall."

"Tonight we're in John, chapter 3. The chapter begins with a religious ruler stating that Jesus must be the Son of God because of His miracles. In verse 3, Jesus responds, 'Verily, verily, I say unto thee, Except a man be born again, he cannot see the kingdom of God.'" Mrs. Hall read from the page in a steady, well-modulated voice.

Mary Ellen raised her hand. "What does that mean, born again? It's not possible."

"That's exactly what Nicodemus said. Look at verse 4. 'Nicodemus saith unto him, How can a man be born when he is old? can he enter the second time into his mother's womb, and be born?'" Mrs. Hall's gaze swept the assembled women and settled on Evelyn, who squirmed. "Nicodemus's question seems logical. It's not like you crawl back inside your mother to be born a second time. And the mothers here are grateful for that." Chuckles filtered from a few of the women. "Let's see how Jesus answered him:

> "*Jesus answered, Verily, verily, I say unto thee, Except a man be born of water and of the Spirit, he cannot enter into the kingdom of God. That which is born of the flesh is flesh; and that which is born of the Spirit is spirit. Marvel not that I said unto thee, Ye must be born again.*'"

"Ah, that makes it so much clearer." A wry smile twisted her lips.

Mary Ellen and a few others looked at Mrs. Hall as if she spoke gibberish, but others nodded.

"I love a later part of this passage." A woman Evelyn knew only by sight spoke. She carried herself through work with confidence and peace. " 'That whosoever believeth in him should not perish, but have everlasting life.' "

"But what does that mean?" Mary Ellen shook her head. "Each time I begin to think I understand, the language confuses me. *Born again. Everlasting life.*" Her forehead wrinkled as she ticked off the terms on her fingers.

Mrs. Hall nodded. "Valid points. Christians tend to use strange language. Almost like you need a special dictionary or interpreter."

Evelyn smiled as others nodded.

"I've always wondered." A woman from a back table shrugged. "I mean, why care about everlasting life? It has to be about more than avoiding hell, a place I'm not convinced exists."

Marjorie caught Mrs. Hall's eye and spoke. "I think the key concept is love. Haven't we all yearned for a love that surrounds us, assures us that we're the most treasured person on earth?" Most of the women nodded. "At times, it feels like love of this sort is a creation of Hollywood or books. But we all want more." She flipped a page in her Bible. "That's what this is all about. See verses 16 and 17? 'For God so loved the world, that he gave his only begotten Son, that whosoever believeth in him should not perish, but have everlasting life. For God sent not his Son into the world to condemn the world; but that the world through him might be saved.'

"That's the good news in two quick sentences. God sent His Son for us because of love. Not for one. Not for a few. But for each of us, individually. Because He doesn't want any of us to die and be separated from Him for the rest of our lives. He longs to save us and can because of what His Son did." Marjorie's eyes glistened, and she paused. "Every time I think of it, I'm humbled and amazed. Who am I that I would be deemed worthy of the love of the God of creation? That He would so long for a relationship with me that He would send His only Son to die for me. The Prince of the universe dying for me, dust."

A hush settled over the room as her words soaked in. Evelyn heard the passion in Marjorie's voice. She felt her heart move within her, responding to something in the words. Truth? Was Marjorie right? She spoke with conviction words that stirred Evelyn—she wanted to believe with the same fervor Marjorie expressed.

"There's so much evil in the world." Marjorie wiped a finger under her eye. "So much evil. Yet there is a love that transcends it all. A love that cleanses of wrongs, forgives sins, and makes us new."

Evelyn wanted to experience that love. To understand and have the relationship Marjorie had. Anything less wouldn't be sufficient. After the meeting ended, she turned to Marjorie, questions pouring from her. "Can I have what you have?"

"Oh yes." Marjorie focused on Evelyn's questions, answering them with a smile and abundance of patience.

"Thank you. You must think I know nothing about faith."

"I don't mind your questions at all." Marjorie looked past Evelyn, as if falling into a memory. "I wouldn't be able to help you if a woman hadn't first taken the time to share her great love for the Father with me. Sometimes, I wonder if she knew how much her kindness and patience would matter in my life."

"And you're sure all it takes is a prayer?" Evelyn couldn't believe it was that simple.

"Think of the prayer as the first step. It gets you on the path to a lifetime of discovery. Every step either leads you closer to the Father or away from Him." She stroked the cover of her Bible. "That's where reading the Bible, praying, and attending church help. Each assists you in hearing His voice and knowing His character."

Evelyn bowed her head. "Jesus, I want to know You. Thank You for dying for me, for covering my sins so I live for You."

Marjorie embraced her, tears trailing her cheeks. "Welcome to the family, Evelyn."

Evelyn nodded, overwhelmed by the idea that she'd

embarked on an adventure of faith. "Me, an engineer."

That night, Evelyn felt a fresh peace as she walked beside Mary Ellen back to her cabin. It was the kind that settled to her bones and let her know that her decision to trust Christ and seek a loving relationship with God had been right.

If only she could bottle this feeling. Pull it out whenever she needed reassurance or had doubts. Tonight, she felt embraced. Felt the burdens, hopes, dreams, and fears she'd carried had transferred to another. She felt the very real presence of the One who loved her completely.

fourteen

August entered with a brace of activity in Building 26 that left Mark wishing for the quieter days of 1942. Yes, it had been frustrating to design a working machine. Now the machines worked more predictably, and the number of WAVES continued to expand from the original seventy to hundreds, all working feverishly on either building components or learning how to operate the machines.

Meader continued to stress that the military needed the machines yesterday. It was a tired song. One Mark never wanted to hear again.

What more could they do? Desch's group tried to strike the balance between the need for machines and the requirement for precision in assembling them.

The lone bright spot in his days was Paige. She'd switched churches so they could spend more time together. Evelyn no longer joined the Millers, claiming to have found a church she enjoyed attending with other WAVES. He hoped she wasn't avoiding seeing him with Paige. The idea left him unsettled. And the thought that he wanted to see Evelyn outside work disturbed him even more.

John waltzed up to him as Mark reached for his hat one sultry evening. "Where do you think you're going at this early hour?"

Mark glanced at the wall clock and shook his head when he read the time. Six o'clock. Hardly an early departure for most people. "I've got an appointment."

John smiled. "Must be meeting Paige. So when are you going to give the gal a ring?"

Evelyn hadn't left yet, and she turned away as if uncomfortable. Mark pondered the question. Paige had hinted she wanted to make their relationship permanent, but the thought still made him a bit uneasy. Until he could identify why, he'd avoid that question.

"Some things a man keeps to himself, John." Mark clapped him on the back. "See you in the morning."

"Yeah, yeah." John's muttering trailed Mark.

The sun shone, warming Mark from the moment he exited Building 26. He headed home to clean up and borrow his dad's car before picking up Paige. Tonight, they'd share a late dinner and maybe a movie. He'd check her mood when he collected her. Since she taught in the morning, she might prefer dinner and dessert.

Mark whistled as he walked into the house.

"Mark?" Mom stuck her head around the corner of the kitchen. "Are you home for dinner?" A pleased smile softened her features.

"Smells good, but not tonight." Mark walked into the kitchen and kissed her cheek.

Her face fell at his words. "You have plans?"

"Picking Paige up. I'll be back later."

"I see." Those two words contained a wealth of information.

"Why don't you like her, Mom?" he shoved his hands in his pockets and leaned against the doorframe. "I've never understood that. She's a Christian. She's beautiful. She wants a family and even likes me. I'd think you'd be crazy about her and the prospect of me settling down."

Mom chewed her lower lip, never a good sign. "It's not that I don't like her."

"But. . ."

"But, I'm not convinced Paige is God's best for you. Is she the woman you can spend the rest of your life with?"

"And she's not Evelyn, right?"

"Why would you say that?"

"You spend so much time with her. But she's not perfect."

His mother stared at him. "What does that mean?"

"She's not a Christian." Mark crossed his arms. What could

she say to that?

A smile creased her face. "That used to be true."

"What?" That wasn't the answer he expected. "She hasn't said anything."

"Not everybody talks about their faith. It's a new decision for her."

"That doesn't change anything." It couldn't, or it might turn his life upside down.

Mom sighed. "You're an adult. If you ask Paige to be your wife and marry her, I'll support you and welcome her into the family. Frankly, I can't explain my hesitation, but it's there."

Mark watched her, wondering if she'd say more. When she didn't, he pushed from the doorframe. "I'm not rushing into anything." Especially not after the news Mom had just unveiled.

"I know." She brushed her hands on a tea towel. "Have a good time."

Mark hurried upstairs, the shadow of his mother's questions and revelation chasing him.

Paige carried the conversation from the moment he picked her up. Teaching left her with a never-ending supply of stories that only required an audience, one he didn't mind providing especially on nights like tonight.

"You should have seen Tommy Custer with that pebble shoved up his nose." She wrinkled hers in disgust, an action Mark found charming. How many people could pull that off? "Where do boys get ideas like that? Before I taught, I would have thought events like that were isolated instances. Now. . ." She shuddered. "I know the truth. Trouble seems programmed into the very nature of little boys. If one tries something, even if it turns out badly, the other boys have to try the same thing."

Mark guffawed. "Just make sure you don't lump me in with the group."

She arched an eyebrow. "What? You didn't do crazy things

like that as a boy? Never caught frogs and put them in the teacher's lunch tin? Never brought the teacher a bouquet of poison ivy—really, who thinks that's a pretty plant?"

"I didn't do anything on that list."

"No, I'm sure you didn't. Instead, you created your own list. Boys are very creative."

Mark parked the car and escorted her into the restaurant. The hostess led them to a table for two in a secluded corner. He enjoyed watching Paige take in their surroundings. He'd wrangled reservations at one of the top restaurants in Dayton, and the look in her eyes made it worth the effort and expense.

He saw the hope in her eyes.

"Is there a special occasion?"

"Do I need one?" How could he head this off before she had them walking down an aisle?

"I guess not." Her look fell a bit. "A girl can wish." She propped her chin on her hand. "So tell me about your day."

"There's nothing much to tell. Same routine."

"Really?" She cocked her head, clearly not believing him. "I'm sure you don't tell that Evelyn 'nothing' about your day."

"That Evelyn?" What a thing to call her. He didn't need an added reason to think about her tonight. Not when his thoughts had cycled back to her all night. He should focus on Paige, but his thoughts refused to cooperate.

Paige toyed with the edge of her menu. "You spend so much time with her. I get the crumbs."

"I work with her." That was it. Why couldn't anyone understand that? Had they all witnessed that almost kiss?

She stared at him with an "of course" look. "That doesn't mean I like it."

"So I should gripe about the men you work with? Worry about what you're doing with them?"

"Don't be ridiculous." She leaned forward on her elbows, staring at him, voice deadly quiet. "They're all married and at least ten years older than me. Nothing for you to worry about. Evelyn, however, is beautiful, intelligent, and you notice."

Mark sat back, blood pumping at her accusation. "Maybe we should leave."

"No. I need you to tell me I'm important. At least as important as your job."

"You are." The words seemed to stick in his throat. He cleared his throat and tried again. "There's no reason to be jealous."

Paige looked away, across the crowded room. The background hum of conversations and clanking dishes swelled in the silence. She smoothed her napkin across her skirt, each fidget making the silence more awkward. "I want to believe you, Mark. But I have no promise from you."

Her words cornered him. He shifted in his seat, Paige's voice warring with his mother's in his mind. "I don't know what to say."

Paige's shoulders slumped, and she hid under the brim of her hat. "You've told me what I needed to know. I'm not so hungry after all." She slid from the booth and stepped into the aisle. "I'll find my way home."

Mark watched her go, then grabbed his hat and jumped to his feet. He threw a dollar on the table, enough to cover their beverages and a tip, and followed her. What had just happened? How had a pleasant night spiraled so quickly into disaster?

He hurried out the front door, intending to offer her a ride home, but spotted her stepping into a cab. "Paige, wait."

She turned his way, one foot in the cab. She smiled sadly and settled into the cab. The restaurant's doorman closed the cab's door. Mark slapped his hat on his head and watched her leave. Uncertainty flooded him. Should he follow her? Did he want to?

❧

Evelyn followed Mary Ellen into the auditorium, relieved to have the excuse to be in a group where her thoughts might focus on something other than the fact that every time she looked up at work Mark was staring at her. She felt uncomfortable around him for the first time in a long time. It didn't help that she'd overheard him tell John that his relationship with Paige looked over.

Tonight's study was the perfect thing to distract her. The group filled a corner of the auditorium, but Marjorie waited for her with an open seat next to her.

Evelyn still had much to learn about her new faith, but the study and Marjorie helped her feel like she was on the right track. She tried to read the Bible on her own each morning, but sometimes the language left her confused and frustrated. It reminded her too much of days in high school trying to decipher Shakespeare. The same Shakespeare that chased her into science and math.

Evelyn listened as the evening's discussion flowed. When it ended, Marjorie turned to her, shadows ringing her eyes.

"Is everything okay?"

"It will be. My daughter Josie's husband has been drafted. I'm not sure what that means for Josie, Cassandra, and little Art Jr. Likely they will come to live with us until he returns. So many are called to serve, leaving families behind." Marjorie rubbed her forehead. "Enough about that. Is work going well? Mark seems buoyed."

Evelyn considered the question. "It is, but not in the way I expected. The problems have moderated. I'm doing what I thought I always wanted, but it doesn't seem so important."

"What do you mean?"

"Working with men, showing them my training is on par with theirs, it doesn't fulfill me like I thought." She shrugged. "But I'm glad I'm here. Someday, we'll know what our work accomplished."

"Ah, the mystery of Building 26." Marjorie smiled.

Evelyn chuckled. "Yes."

"Is there any way I can pray for you?"

"That I'd understand what God wants from me." Evelyn studied her long fingers. "Living a life of faith is confusing."

"A mystery we see only dimly. I'll pray for you, and this is the kind of prayer God loves to answer."

"Why?"

"Because you're asking to have a deeper understanding of God's purpose for you. How you follow Him in all you do."

Evelyn considered Marjorie's words. "I guess that is what I'm asking. This is still so new to me."

"And the beautiful thing about the journey of faith is that it will always have a freshness to it." Marjorie's tired eyes brightened. "His mercies are new every morning. I am so grateful it's true. I'll need to remember that in the coming months."

"Any idea where Josie's husband is going?"

"We think Art will be assigned to the European theater." Marjorie hunched forward. "Time will tell." She smiled, small and tight. "I'm grateful God is not limited to certain continents and places. Well, I need to head home, see Mr. Miller." Marjorie stood, then paused. "Join us for lunch Sunday?"

"I'd like that, but I've found a new church to attend."

"That's fine. How about we pick you up for lunch on our way home?"

Evelyn nodded, the thought of a meal with the Millers filling her with joy and a bit of uncertainty.

&

The next week, rumors filtered through Building 26 that the Allies' recent success against U-boats might be related to their work. The thought energized Evelyn. Victory on the European front only became possible when supplies and men could safely cross the Atlantic.

While many pieces came together to ease the Allied losses, the longer-range B-24 airplane certainly played a role. But Evelyn hoped the rumors were correct and something they did in Building 26 had helped.

During the early days of August, the Bombes decrypted messages at increasingly faster rates. One morning, Lt. Meyers sent a message, summoning Evelyn to her small office. Evelyn couldn't decide whether to be excited or apprehensive. As far as she knew, she hadn't done anything worthy of a reprimand, but she couldn't be sure what the navy would focus on.

Evelyn rapped on the lieutenant's door.

"Come in."

"Ensign Happ reporting." She entered the room and paused when she saw Admiral Meader seated at the lieutenant's desk. "Sir?"

"Have a seat, Ensign." Lt. Meyers gestured to a chair in front of her desk.

Evelyn perched on the edge of the seat.

Admiral Meader observed her, the silence resting heavy. "Ensign Happ, you've participated on the project here how long?"

"Since May, sir. Came with the first WAVES."

He flipped open a file on the desk. "We've decided to reassign you."

"Reassign me?"

He arched an eyebrow in her direction. "Is there a problem with that?"

"No, sir."

"We're in the beginning stages of a new project, and with your background and experience working with the machines, you are the perfect candidate."

"Yes, sir." Evelyn reminded herself when she enlisted she'd given control of her life to the navy. However, Admiral Meader's cryptic nothings annoyed her.

Lt. Meyers watched the exchange, nodding her head.

"Ensign, you're perfect for this assignment. The lieutenant has full confidence in your ability. I know you'd like to know more, Ensign, but you'll know it on a need-to-know basis. All you need to know now is that your days here are numbered."

fifteen

When Evelyn returned to Adam's room, Mark noticed how quiet she was. She sank into a chair and gently shook her head.

Mark eased into a chair next to her. "Good meeting?"

She stared at Adam as if she hadn't heard a word.

"You okay?"

"Hmm?" Evelyn shook her head slightly. "Everything's fine." The machine clicked to a stop before the gears backed up. "Jackpot. Did you believe we'd accomplish this?"

"What?"

"Breaking a code as complex as the Germans'?"

Mark watched John pull the print out from the machine and take it to the Enigma. "Yeah, I did. Given enough time, American ingenuity would win out. It took a lot of work, though."

"What next?" Evelyn turned to him, the force of her gray eyes connecting with his made him hold his breath.

"I'll be here through the war."

"Must be nice." She must have read the question on his face because she hurried to continue. "To know what you're doing."

"It's a jackpot, boys and girl!" John crowed.

"Time for a break." Mark offered his hand to help Evelyn from her chair. "Let's get something to drink."

"As long as it's not the cafeteria's coffee."

Mark purchased a Coke for each of them; then they headed outside. Large, flatbed train cars stood on the railroad spur behind Building 26. They hadn't been there the day before. "Wonder what they're getting ready to transport."

"We may never know." Frustration crept into her voice and

the set of her shoulders.

Mark searched for a change of topic. Whatever had happened in the meeting had Evelyn on edge, and she seemed unwilling or unable to tell him. "Mom said you're coming for dinner Sunday."

"Yes, though if it's easier, I can go to church with you."

"I'll let Mom know." They walked down the road a bit. "Mom enjoys your friendship."

"I enjoy it, too. She's changed my life. I'll never forget the way she's guided me to faith."

"Mom loves to answer questions."

"But it's more than that. She's good at answers. She knows what I'm thinking before I do and reaches the heart of my questions."

The only sound was that of the birds singing from a few trees. Evelyn's face had settled into an uncustomary frown. "That meeting must have been something else."

She turned toward him. "Why?"

"The confident, vivacious woman I've come to know and admire has disappeared. You are daring and fun. Someone others enjoy being around, and now you look knocked back on your heels."

"But I'm not Paige, right?" Her hand covered her mouth as if to prevent other words from escaping.

"I don't compare you to Paige." At least not more than every few hours.

Evelyn studied him then shook her head. "So you say." She took the last sip from her bottle. "We need to head back before they send the MPs. Thank you for the Coke." A shadow of a smile softened her features.

Her comment chased him that night. Paige had removed herself from his life. He couldn't blame her. His inability to commit had finally frustrated her. He hoped she met the man who would knock her off her feet. She'd probably been too patient. But now he had to confront the reality that he cared for Evelyn. In a way that didn't make sense. In a way he couldn't articulate. In a way he couldn't admit.

Mark made a point over the next few days of spending breaks with Evelyn. Something still bothered her, and as they enjoyed time together, he held his feelings for her in check. She remained oblivious to what he felt or ignored it. Still, he lived for the moments she laughed at something he said. The shadows disappeared, and the old Evelyn would reappear.

Sunday, she joined his family for church and lunch. Instead of watching the service as an observer, she participated. He hid a smile as she took notes in a slim notebook. It was as if every word from the pastor watered her thirsty soul. When had he soaked in the sermon like that? He didn't know, but he felt challenged to focus on his personal walk.

While Paige had shared his faith, he'd never felt the challenge to take his faith deeper because of time with her. The thought of her still brought a pang. Investing so much time in a person to have nothing come of it was painful, but he'd acknowledged something the night Paige left him at the restaurant. She wasn't the right woman for him. He'd known it but had buried that knowledge deep in his heart.

The following week, their breaks continued, with Evelyn relaxing more in his company. Whatever had kept her tense the prior week disappeared.

Evelyn looked at him over another Coke. At the rate he purchased the drink, maybe he should buy stock in the company.

"Do you miss her?"

"Who?"

She rolled her eyes. "Paige."

"I miss her crazy stories about her kids' antics in class. But, no. I don't regret spending my time with you rather than her."

She quirked an eyebrow at him as if she couldn't quite believe him.

"You understand parts of me that Paige never bothered to try. And you make me want to pursue my relationship with Christ." He took a breath, then wiped a tear from her cheek. "Believe me?"

"I'm trying to."

That would have to be enough until he could convince her she could rely on his word.

The first Bombes shipped to DC after being loaded onto railroad cars late at night. Mark and John had hefted a carefully packed box loaded down with rotors and connections and carried it toward the cars. They stopped when they saw the sailors with guns guarding the train.

"I guess they're taking this seriously."

"Deadly." Mark shifted his hold on the box.

John struggled with his end. "Watch it, Miller."

They strained to get the box on the train and hurried out of the way of the next box-toting pair. The night passed quickly, and Mark was grateful when the last box found its way to the train.

&

August melted into September. Though Evelyn waited for any word of her new assignment, nothing came of the meeting with Admiral Meader. She stopped looking over her shoulder, pulling away from the people around her as she waited to be shipped out to points unknown.

It helped that Mark spent so much time with her. At his invitation, she'd rejoined the Millers for church and Sunday lunches. She enjoyed the time with them and the opportunity to learn more about her new faith. One thing she'd learned was that her faith didn't make life smooth and perfect. It made the bumps on the road easier to navigate. She welcomed the peace that flowed through her days.

Marjorie continued to answer her questions, but each of Marjorie's answers generated three new questions. She hoped the woman's patience endured as she continued to monopolize Marjorie's time on Sunday afternoons.

One morning, Mark bounced into the workroom. He strode up to Evelyn, spun her around, and dipped her. She laughed at the sudden moves as her pulse raced at the warmth of his arms holding her. "Good morning to you, too." She couldn't think while he had her tipped over. "What's the special occasion?"

He eased her back to a standing position, and his touch lingered on her arms. "Come with us this weekend to watch Kat play a couple of games."

"Join who where?" He didn't make sense, but she loved the delighted grin on his face.

"My family. We're going to South Bend where Kat and her team are playing for the weekend." He waggled his eyebrows at her. "Join us. It'll be well chaperoned, and you'll have a great time getting away from Dayton."

"Who's 'us'?" She couldn't simply take his word on chaperones, after all. She had the WAVES image to uphold.

"Josie, her kids Cassandra and Art Jr., Mom, Dad, and yours truly." A rakish air fell over him. "You know it'll be better than any plans you could have here. Who wouldn't want a weekend surrounded by the Millers?"

She laughed. "You can be persuasive, you know that, Mark?"

"Of course."

Evelyn eased back from the circle of his arms. Her thoughts were muddled with him holding her around the waist. "Fine."

"Yes?"

"Yes. Though I have to warn you I know nothing about softball other than what I've learned from watching a couple of games at Sugar Camp."

"I'll explain it to you. We'll pick you up at six, Friday evening."

Once he had her agreement, Mark morphed into the engineer she knew. The week flew while she questioned her sanity in agreeing to go. Wouldn't a weekend excursion create more confusion with Mark?

And why did she care?

Although things had ended between Mark and Paige, that didn't mean he was free. Evelyn could list dozens of reasons they shouldn't be more than colleagues. He valued her contributions to the team, often being the first to suggest her approach be attempted. He didn't seem to care what she looked like, yet the fire of attraction sparked between them anytime they got too close. Besides, what would happen if Admiral Meader followed through with reassigning her?

Guess it was a good thing the WAVES controlled her destiny since she didn't know what she wanted anymore.

No, that wasn't true.

She wanted Mark to see her as a woman. All the time.

๛

Mark tossed Josie's bag in his trunk.

Life would be a bit complicated as they headed to South Bend for the game, but he thought he'd wrangled it so that only Evelyn would travel with him. Maybe Cassandra would join them, but how much trouble could a twelve-year-old be?

Josie and her little boy, Art Jr., climbed into the backseat of Dad's vehicle. Dad walked up to Mark. "You have the map, son?"

"Yes, sir. We'll be a few minutes behind you."

"We'll connect at the hotel. Josie and the kids can share a room with Evelyn." His dad studied him a moment. "Be careful."

Mark had the distinct impression his father's caution referred to more than his driving Josie's car. Cassandra hopped into the passenger seat, a big grin on her face.

"Ready for the adventure, Cassie?"

She wrinkled her nose and stuck out her tongue. "As soon as you quit calling me that. My given name is Cassandra."

He chucked her under the chin. "Nice to see your pep is intact. Let's go get our guest." A few minutes later they pulled up to Sugar Camp. He'd barely reached her cabin when the door opened and Evelyn came out with a small bag.

Mark took it from her. "Are you ready for a great weekend?"

"Yes." A shy smile graced her lips. "Thanks again for inviting me. I could hardly wait for you to get here."

Cassandra greeted Evelyn and slipped into the backseat with a pout.

As they drove, the sky eventually darkened. The headlights

made twin pillars across the pavement. Mark turned on the radio, and Evelyn sang with some of the tunes, her voice a sweet accompaniment. Mark felt settled and at peace even as the miles seemed to lengthen.

"Are we there?" Cassandra had asked the question repeatedly since the twilight had forced an end to her reading. "I can't sit another moment."

Evelyn turned toward her. "Look at all the lights clustered on the horizon. I bet we're close."

"I hope so."

"Close your eyes, Cassandra. The time will go faster." Evelyn leaned her head against the seat and turned her attention to Mark. "Tell me more about your time at MIT."

She'd peppered him for stories during the drive, and he'd cajoled a few stories of Purdue from her. They may have shared majors, but the schools couldn't have been more different. One urban, the other rural. He shrugged.

"There's not much. Study, class, study again."

"There must have been a girl." Her words fell soft in the space between them.

Something told him to tread carefully. "I took girls out on occasion, but no one serious."

"Really?"

"Yes."

"Hmm."

"Why's that so hard to believe?"

"I don't know. You seem the type to work hard, but also have fun." She paused. "At least before this assignment."

"Building 26 does drain one's energy." He tapped the steering wheel as they pulled into the outskirts of South Bend. "That's why everyone should have a weekend like this."

Evelyn laughed, a sound he wanted to tease from her again and again. "I didn't know I needed it, but I'm determined to enjoy it." She turned to look at him. "Thank you for including me."

"You're welcome." He studied her silhouette before turning

back to the road. "So how about you? Any special guys?" He cringed. Why ask that? It would only make him look like a fool.

An awkward silence made him regret his question.

"No." She shrugged. "It never worked."

Cassandra sighed. "Can't you talk about anything but school and romance?" Disgust laced her voice. "I should have ridden in the other car."

Evelyn burst out laughing. "Out of the mouths of babes."

"I'm not a babe."

"I stand corrected." Evelyn looked at Mark, and he thought she winked. "We'll keep our conversation to more mundane matters. Do you have anything in mind?"

"Movie stars. Don't you think Cary Grant is amazing?" Cassandra swooned against the seat.

Evelyn kept Cassandra entertained but left Mark wondering who held her heart. It mattered very much.

sixteen

The weekend passed in a blur, one that Evelyn thoroughly enjoyed. Being surrounded by Mark's family wrapped around her like a blanket of acceptance. The love that flowed between them included her.

Kat didn't get to spend much time with them. Instead, her time was consumed with her team and the games. But the meal she joined held a new level of affection and teasing. Her vivacious personality rubbed off on everyone else, and Cassandra mimicked her every move and speech patterns, though tinged with her accent. The British child charmed Kat's teammates and quickly became their pet.

Evelyn tried to enjoy the games but found it hard to focus. She wanted to believe it was because she didn't understand the rules. Honesty forced her to acknowledge the man next to her provided the distraction.

She'd been attracted to her growing faith because of the example of his mother. Watching him at work each day had only reinforced her desire to see if she could share it. He worked hard but never let the frustrations wear him down, even when another failed attempt disappointed him. He'd managed to keep a light tone most days despite the constant pressure from Admiral Meader and Mr. Desch.

"Ready to head back?"

Evelyn turned to Mark, wondering how long he'd tried to get her attention. "I think we should become Blossoms followers. Trail them on the road."

Mark laughed then stretched his back. "I don't think I can handle the time on a bleacher." He twisted from side to side. "How did Mom attend my games over the years?"

"Lots of love."

"Touché." He stood. "How about another round of Cracker Jacks before we leave?"

"Add a Coke too, and I'm in."

"Back in a minute." Mark grinned at her before disappearing up the stairs and out to the concession stand.

Marjorie scooted closer to her. "Having a good time?"

"Yes." Evelyn tried to force her features into a neutral expression, but the look in Marjorie's eyes indicated she'd failed. Miserably.

"When will the two of you quit being stubborn and admit your feelings for each other?"

Evelyn flushed at the direct question. "I don't know what you're talking about."

Marjorie leaned onto her arms and looked at Evelyn. "Really? I'll remember that next time I watch two people I care about avoid the truth."

"You're wrong."

"I see. Is that why you're very aware of my son?" Marjorie scooted closer and nudged Evelyn's shoulder. "Here's a life secret."

"Okay." This should be interesting.

"God cares deeply about the things that matter to you." Marjorie nodded. "It's a wonderful part about being a Christian. The things that bother and worry us can be turned over to Him with the assurance He sees and cares."

Evelyn shook her head. "He's the Creator of the universe. I doubt He cares about whether I marry and whom."

"*Au contraire*, darling. In fact, He wants us to pray about the matters in our lives. To turn them over to Him and His leading." The sound of Cassandra and Art Jr. jostling and joking with Mark reached them, and Marjorie turned to watch them. "While I might have a preference about how things turn out, God has your best interests at heart. And He wants to be your number-one focus. Seek Him, and everything else can fall into place."

Evelyn considered her words. "I have so much to learn."

"And a lifetime to figure it out."

"Special delivery for the ladies." Mark slipped into the row. "Cracker Jacks and Coke." He looked from one woman to the other. "What did I miss?"

"Nothing." Evelyn tried to smile as she took a box of Cracker Jacks and bottle of Coke. "Thank you."

The game continued around her, but Evelyn couldn't focus on it. Marjorie's words pursued her.

❧

Mark tried to pull Evelyn out of her introspective mood, but she insisted everything was okay. He settled on the bench beside her and soon coached her through softball's rules again.

Kat was a dynamo all over the infield, but he couldn't take full pleasure in that while puzzling over the woman next to him.

"Evelyn?" He touched her hand, and she jumped as if he'd trailed a lit firecracker along her arm rather than his fingers. "Are you having a good time?"

"Absolutely." A smile curved her lips. Before he was ready, the game ended, signaling the end of the weekend.

When they reached the parking lot, Cassandra opted to join Josie and the Millers for the drive back, leaving Mark and Evelyn to travel alone. The easy conversation that filled the car on the drive to Indiana reappeared as they headed back to Dayton.

After an hour, Mark's stomach growled, and Evelyn giggled. "Not enough Cracker Jacks?"

"Guess not." Mark tapped his hands on the steering wheel. "Let's stop for dinner."

Mark pulled the car into the parking lot of a small diner. He opened her door and led her inside. A waitress seated them in a booth and took his burger order. Evelyn stared at the mound of food on his plate. "I'm glad I didn't order anything. You'd need all day to eat that by yourself."

Mark stared at the burger and mound of French fries and

grinned. "Guess you'll have to help me."

She snapped up a fry and ran it through the pile of ketchup. An easy silence surrounded them as he ate. Mark chewed his last bite and then swallowed. "Would you like to go on a date? When we get back to Dayton? I mean, not tonight, of course, but some other time." Where was a cork when he needed one? He threw money on the table for their meal and tip, then pulled her to her feet. "Let's get back on the road."

Evelyn stared at him like she'd never seen him before. "What?"

"Time to finish this drive."

"Not that."

"Could I take you to dinner? Maybe a movie? Not a spur-of-the-moment, grab-a-bite after work, but an intentioned time with you."

"You see me most Sundays."

"I want to spend more time getting to know you apart from my family. When you're at our house, you spend your time with my mother. Don't get me wrong. That's wonderful. I love watching you probe your relationship with God. But I'd like to spend more time like we had this weekend. Alone. Getting to know each other."

She put a finger on his lips, stopping the words he intended to say.

"Don't say it, unless you mean it. Words are too easy to have meaning without action."

He stared into her eyes, their gray color picking up the hint of purple in the dusky sky. "If my words aren't enough, I don't know what else I can offer."

He opened her car door, but stopped her before she climbed in. Mark took Evelyn's face in his hands and placed his forehead on hers. "I would never do anything to hurt you."

Her eyes searched his, measuring his words. She licked her lips. "Those are just words, Mark."

Words? Then he'd act. He lowered his lips and claimed

hers in a kiss. Evelyn stiffened a moment then relaxed. He held her smooth cheeks lightly with his hands, then started to pull back, when a honk caused him to jerk away from Evelyn.

Her eyes stayed closed a moment before she opened them and slid into the passenger seat. Mark pulled the car onto the highway, a soft silence between them. How could he tell her the kiss meant something, that he didn't kiss every girl he spent time with, without offending her like he had after the infamous almost kiss. He had to try. "Evelyn, you're an amazing woman. I hope you know what just happened means something."

He tore his gaze from the road long enough to gauge whether the words impacted her.

Evelyn stared out the side window, her face difficult to see. "It did for me, too."

The miles slid beneath the car's tires. Before long, Evelyn started regaling him with stories of her life in Washington. As he listened, Mark couldn't imagine how their backgrounds could be more different. She grew up having senators and ambassadors join the family for dinner. Occasionally, his dad brought home a grad student or fellow professor, but nothing as intimidating as a senator.

As he listened, he wondered if she could be content to spend the rest of her life in a place like Dayton. If not, could he abandon a life he loved for the woman he loved? Even after he dropped Evelyn off at Sugar Camp, the questions plagued him, easy answers nowhere in sight.

The next weeks wove together in the routine of building new machines and having coffee breaks with Evelyn. Their friendship grew, built on mugs of coffee. Sunday afternoons were filled with walks and conversations, ever deepening yet cautious. Evelyn held him at arm's length as if afraid what they had couldn't last.

The weather turned colder, and October rains fell. Mark started riding home with a colleague to avoid the soaking rain. Anthony Gutling was quiet and kept to himself, the perfect companion at the end of a shift. One afternoon, Mark reached the car before Anthony and opened the passenger door to wait inside the relative warmth of the vehicle.

When he climbed in, his knees banged into the glove compartment, and the door opened. Mark groaned as bundles of papers spilled out. Nothing to do but stick them back inside.

"Evening, Mark," John Fields bellowed as he strode across the parking lot toward the bus stop.

Mark waved and turned back to his task. He groped along the floor and shoved papers back into the small compartment. He grabbed a stack of 3 x 5 cards. Flipping through them to see if they were in order, he paused. They contained neatly typed lists of German and Japanese individuals and organizations. Why would Anthony have these? Mark slipped them into the compartment.

Bending over, he felt under the seat and pulled out the last piece of paper. The paper felt thicker. The document opened to reveal an official seal. Mark couldn't resist scanning it. He blinked when he read the first few lines. A letter from the German embassy?

The embassy stated it could not fulfill Anthony's request. No good reason existed to contact the German embassy. Not now. A knot tightened in Mark's stomach. What should he do with this? The Germans couldn't find out about the activities in Building 26, but the letter made it clear Anthony was in contact with them.

Had he successfully communicated with the Germans before? Or was this Anthony's first attempt?

The ramifications spiraled through Mark's mind, leaving him shaken.

How to handle this?

Mark jumped from the car, paper still firmly gripped in his hand. Beads of sweat lined his brow. Start with Desch? Find Admiral Meader? Go straight to the MPs? He needed wisdom, and the navy needed this information.

"You headed somewhere?"

Mark startled and looked up to see Anthony Gutling staring at him. He'd been so caught up in his thoughts he'd missed the approach of footsteps.

"I left something in the building."

"Do you want me to wait for you?" A curious light filled Anthony's eyes. Did he suspect?

"No. That's all right. I'll walk home or catch a ride with someone else. Thanks anyway." Mark hurried back to Building 26, hoping Anthony couldn't make out the paper he still clutched. He should have shoved it in his briefcase.

As soon as he reached the building, Mark looked for Desch. He would know what to do with this information. Mark's blood pounded in his ears as he hurried down long hallways. He finally stopped one of the marines strolling the halls.

"Have you seen Joe Desch?"

The man stared through him. "No, sir."

"How about Admiral Meader?"

"Negative."

Mark grunted. He had to find them.

"I think they went home for the evening."

Then that's where Mark needed to go. Thirty minutes later, the cab he'd hailed pulled up in front of the Desches' modest home. Mark paid the man, then charged to the door. He pounded on it, more than ready to pass the incriminating document on to someone else. Let someone above his pay grade determine the best way to handle the situation.

Mrs. Desch opened the door, dressed in a simple housecoat very different from her stylish attire during the events the Desches hosted. "Yes?"

"Mrs. Desch, you probably don't remember me, but I'm Mark Miller. I'm sorry to disturb you at this hour, but I work for your husband and need to talk to him. Now."

She must have heard the intensity in his voice, because she

stepped aside. "Yes, of course. Come in." She led him to a small living room, where her husband played checkers on the floor with a small girl.

Desch looked up at Mark, a question in his eyes.

"Sir, I need a moment of your time. I'm hoping you can advise me on a sensitive matter."

"Of course. Debbie, we'll finish our game later."

"Come along with me, darling." Mrs. Desch gestured for the child to stand. The little girl obeyed and followed her mother to the hallway.

Once they left the room, Desch took a seat on the davenport. He pointed Mark to the club chair. "What's on your mind?"

"I've been riding home with another employee."

Desch put one foot against his other knee. "Yes?"

"Today when I got to the car before him, I found this." Mark handed the sheet over, and Desch scanned the page. Furrows formed between his eyebrows. Without a word, the man bolted to his feet and headed out of the room. Mark remained seated, unsure what to do next. He heard a pounding off the hallway, and shifted in his chair.

A minute later, Admiral Meader hurried into the room, Desch on his heels. "Where did you find this?"

"In a fellow employee's vehicle."

"Were you snooping?"

"No, sir. It fell out of the glove compartment. When I picked it up I noticed it was addressed to the German embassy. I knew that wasn't good news."

"Does the man know that you have this?" Meader's eyes pierced Mark, as if determined to ferret out whether he told the truth.

Mark's mouth dried up, and he tried to swallow. "No, sir, I don't believe so."

"Which is it? Yes or no?"

"I don't think he knows."

Meader settled back on the couch. "All right. Joe, would you call our guards in?"

A storm cloud gathered on Desch's brow. "You know I hate their presence."

Meader stared at Desch. Mark stiffened, uncertain what would happen in the battle of wills between the two. "Do you want me to get them?" Not that he knew where they were, but he could find them.

"No." Meader turned to him, a grave look weighing his face. "You'll talk to them in due course."

Mark didn't know what to expect, but the grilling he received in the following hours was not it. The navy security and Admiral Meader wanted to know again and again how he'd come to have the paper, how long he had known Gutling, and answers to more questions than he could answer.

His brain felt mushy, and he wondered if he could keep his answers straight. Telling the truth shouldn't be so hard, especially when he'd done nothing wrong. But as he sat in the living room being interrogated by three navy men in suits while Admiral Meader and Desch watched, he was the one under fire.

seventeen

A pall hung over Building 26 when Evelyn reported for duty the next morning. Security to get into the building and into Adam's room was tighter. More marines and MPs walked the halls and checked IDs.

A knot formed in her stomach and didn't ease as she hung her hat and purse on a hook at the back of the room. Adam chugged through another search, but even that sound held ominous overtones. John Fields watched the machine, but Mark didn't work next to him.

"Where's Mark?"

The bulky man shrugged. "Nobody'll say. But it's not like him to be absent."

Evelyn had to agree. In the months she'd worked in Dayton, Mark hadn't missed one day. The man was as committed to his job as anyone, even on the days he should be in bed. He'd looked fine yesterday, so she doubted poor health kept him away.

Mr. Desch strode into the room, dark circles rimming his eyes. "Ensign Happ, a word."

The knot tightened and her head began to pound. "Yes, sir."

She followed him from the room, down several hallways, and to the offices. The sun streaming through the glass walls failed to warm her.

An MP opened the door, a scowl replacing the usually blank expression. Evelyn gulped and looked at Mr. Desch.

She took a step forward, and the door closed behind her. Admiral Meader sat behind a broad desk, with a man standing on either side of him. "Please have a seat, Ensign."

Evelyn eased into a seat, and noticed Lt. Meyers standing against the back wall. The woman's usually warm expression

136

had hardened. What had happened? Whispers of panic trailed down her spine. She kept her posture stiff and perched on the edge of the seat.

"Ensign Happ, we have a few questions for you. I admonish you to carefully consider your answers."

"Do. . .do I need an attorney?"

"Have you done anything wrong?"

For the life of her, Evelyn couldn't think of a solitary thing. She glanced at Lt. Meyers, but the officer gave her no indication how she should respond. Evelyn shook her head.

"Good." Admiral Meader picked up a pad of paper. "You have been accused of spying."

Evelyn's jaw dropped. Panic colored her vision. Spying? Her mind couldn't embrace the word, could barely comprehend it. The word was harsh. And in a world at war, the word contained a death sentence. She swallowed and tried to form words. "I don't understand." Such a weak thing to say.

"One of your colleagues has implicated you in an attempt to contact the German embassy."

"I would never do that. I haven't done that."

"Doesn't your family frequently entertain?"

"My family?" What could her family have to do with this accusation?

"Your father is Archibald Happ, industrial lobbyist." He stated the words, but she nodded anyway.

"Yes. It's in my application."

"And in that capacity, your parents frequently entertain dignitaries." The words had a harsh edge that left Evelyn with little doubt where this line of questioning would lead. Yet she couldn't deny the truth, so nodded.

"And German embassy staff attended often."

"I suppose so." How could she make him understand that she couldn't keep track of everyone who attended? Her parents enjoyed the events far more than she did, all the talk of politics boring her endlessly. And it had been over a year. "I haven't attended one in a long time."

Everything from the tilt of his chin to the arch in his brow indicated he did not believe her. What could she do?

"Sir, I am a patriotic American who has enlisted to better serve her country. I would do nothing to compromise the missions of my country, especially one as important as this project."

"Yes, yet you managed to get around security and into Adam's room several times before being added to the list."

"I. . .yes."

"Why? Were you searching for information you could pass on to the Germans or Italians?"

"No!"

"If not, what was your purpose?" Admiral Meader leaned halfway across his desk. Evelyn refused to give an inch even though she wanted to shrink against the chair.

Her voice rose to meet his. "I wanted to be part of something bigger. Something that would impact the course of the war. It does not take someone with my background and training to understand the implications of the project housed here. We can impact this war. We already are." How else would the war in the Atlantic have shifted so dramatically? "I would never do anything to compromise anything so important to the security of my country and the safety of her fighting men."

Meader settled back in his chair. "That's what I expected you to say. You're dismissed, Ensign."

Evelyn eased from her seat, noticing Meader looking at someone hidden in the shadows.

"Well, Miller?" he barked.

Evelyn turned and stiffened when she noticed Mark Miller sitting in a corner. Everything warm in her body fled at the sight of him sitting there. Her accuser?

Evelyn flew from the room, and Mark rushed to catch up with her. "Evelyn, wait."

❧

Evelyn rushed on as if she hadn't heard him. He could only imagine what she thought after the way Meader had set him up. Mark had played right into his hands, and now Evelyn must be furious and hurt. He knew the pain he'd feel if it appeared she'd accused him.

Mark picked up his pace until he caught up with her. He grabbed her arm, pulling her to a stop. She bounced against his chest, then looked at him, gray eyes blazing.

"I never want to see you again, Mr. Miller."

"Let me explain."

Evelyn stared at him before turning back down the hall. She was poised to take off, and he couldn't let that happen. He needed her to understand what had really happened. She shook off his hand, so he hurried in front of her and grabbed her by the shoulders.

"Listen to me." His words huffed from his mouth, more forceful than he'd intended. He hung his head. When he looked up, tears hung in her eyes like crystals. Her lips were parted, and her cheeks had emptied of color. The pain in her expression pierced his heart. He leaned down and kissed her. The moment his lips touched hers, the world felt right again. This was the woman he loved. He deepened the kiss. She stopped squirming and a small sound escaped her throat. He pulled her closer, wanting to comfort her, then took a step back, placing his forehead on hers. "Evelyn."

One word. Yet it said everything. She had worked her way into his heart, and he couldn't imagine her anywhere else.

A hard hand slapped his cheek. The burning sensation sparked with pain. He pulled back and rubbed it. "What was that for?"

"You. . .have. . .no. . .right." The words spit from her mouth. "Good-bye, Mr. Miller."

❧

Evelyn hurried away from Mark. She needed to go somewhere, anywhere, to get away from him and this hideous building. Sobs hiccupped in her chest, but she forced them down. No one could see her pain. Despite her best efforts, she'd been betrayed by another man. She'd tried so hard to guard her heart but had allowed Mark under her defenses. What a fool! She knew better. And now, when her heart belonged to him, he'd handed her over as a spy.

She'd imagined the next time Mark would kiss her.

Never had she dreamed it would be in the face of his betrayal.

Oh God. The name rose like a prayer in her mind. She didn't know what else to say. Wasn't life supposed to be easier once one became a Christian? She'd never felt such pain. That kiss should have been filled with the promise of so much more. Instead, it emphasized the depths of his betrayal.

Evelyn escaped into the cafeteria, relieved to find it empty of patrons at this odd time of the morning. Too late for breakfast, too early for coffee breaks. She found a chair facing away from the door and collapsed into it. What could she do? Her mind pulsed with random ideas and questions, but she fought to pull them together into any sort of coherent plan.

"Mind if I join you?" The quiet voice caused Evelyn to turn. Lt. Meyers seemed to take that as agreement and sat at the table. "Ensign Happ, we had to interview you."

Evelyn bit back her protests.

"You gained access to a room you shouldn't have. More than once." Lt. Meyers raised her hand. "Yes, we know there were reasons each time. Still, you got in. We have to explore all avenues, even the ones we aren't convinced are right."

"What happens now?"

"You'll get a day or two off and report back to work." Lt. Meyers smiled, though it failed to reach her eyes. "You might as well enjoy them. Soon enough, you'll work long shifts again."

"What if I don't want to stay?"

The officer's eyes narrowed. "Don't forget you are a WAVES who took an oath to serve where the navy decides you are needed." Her words hung in the air. "For now, head back to Sugar Camp. I'll let you know when to return."

The next three days passed in a haze of inactivity. Each morning, Viv, Lonnie, and Mary Ellen got ready for work and left while Evelyn remained behind. Evelyn didn't know how to explain her absence to them. As soon as the others left, she pulled out her Bible and a notebook. She tried to occupy her days with study and long walks filled with prayer. A puzzling peace carried her through the uncertainty and pain. Each night, Viv brought messages from Mark, but Evelyn couldn't face him, not yet. She wasn't ready to discuss what happened. Neither the kiss nor the betrayal to Admiral Meader. Someday, she'd need to hear his side, but not yet.

By Thursday night, Evelyn had decided if she spent another day in her cabin she'd go crazy. In addition to her Bible, she'd read three books in three days, a new record. By the time Viv walked into the cabin carrying a bouquet of sunflowers, Evelyn had read the same page in *Pride and Prejudice* for twenty minutes.

The bright blooms brought a smile to her face. Evelyn tossed the book to the side. "Who sent you those?"

"Oh, they aren't for me." Viv tightened her grip on the vase. "Not that I wouldn't love them. These beauties are for you."

Evelyn reached for the vase, but Viv didn't let go.

"I thought they were for me."

Viv groaned, then released the flowers. "You're a lucky woman. Extra days off and now flowers. I'd love to receive flowers from a guy smitten with me."

"I doubt whoever sent them is taken."

Viv snorted. "They say you're a smart woman? You are so nearsighted."

Evelyn took the flowers, setting them on the bedside table. A slim card hid in the bouquet. She pulled it out, hands trembling when she saw the name of the sender: Mark.

When Lonnie brought the word later that Mark waited at the cafeteria for her, Evelyn stalled.

"Are you trying to chase a good man away?" Lonnie fisted her hands on her hips.

Mary Ellen handed her a tube of lipstick. "You might want this first."

Evelyn needed to face him. Hear his side of the story. Even if it was uncomfortable. "I'm leaving."

"Oh no you don't." Viv handed her a brush. "Not before you beautify."

One glance in the mirror had Evelyn racing for the brush and lipstick. Four days of lounging while her work waited hadn't done her any favors. Ten minutes later, she crossed the camp. A whisper of air teased her neck. She shivered and quickened her pace. Mark waited on the cafeteria's front porch. He straightened and hustled down the steps.

"Evelyn." His voice caressed her bruised heart.

She stilled in front of him. Evelyn wanted to rail against his deception but held her words in check. The tentative look in his eyes made her want to forgive him. "I thought you were my friend."

"I am."

"A friend doesn't malign someone like you did!" Her chin quivered despite her efforts to still it. Heat rose up her neck as she noticed WAVES stopping and staring.

Mark touched her elbow and led her toward the parking lot. What rumors would fly around Sugar Camp after her outburst?

"I need to explain what happened." Steel lay under Mark's words. "I didn't know Admiral Meader would interrogate you."

He didn't? Then why had he sat in the room during her inquisition? "I don't understand."

Mark opened the passenger door to his dad's car and helped her in. After he climbed in, he turned to face her. "You arrived before they dismissed me. They forgot about me." He ran his fingers through his hair. "How much have they told you?"

"Just what you heard. I don't even know when I get to come back to Building 26." And she didn't know that she wanted to anymore. Her fellow WAVES had picked up on the strange treatment she'd received and that she hadn't reported to work even though she wasn't sick. Why couldn't a cold have coincided with her forced break?

"I don't know what I can tell you." Mark's grim tone made clear his frustration.

Evelyn dredged up the courage to ask the question that had haunted her. "Do they think I'm a spy?"

"They can't. Not seriously."

"Your enthusiastic support is encouraging."

Mark slipped the key into the ignition and pulled out of his parking spot. "They haven't told me much since Monday." He turned out of Sugar Camp and seemed to drive without a destination in mind.

Evelyn peeked at her watch when they passed through the light from a street lamp. Almost 10:30. "You'll have to get me back soon. They've changed the curfew."

"I thought no one enforced it."

"It's tightened since whatever you uncovered developed." Evelyn covered her face with her hands. "They can't believe I'm a spy."

If they did, everything she had worked so hard for would disappear. She had thought becoming a Christian would make life easier, but she hadn't found any verses that supported that idea. Instead, she'd found verses about trouble filling the world. Yet God promised peace that surpassed all understanding. And in the midst of the week and its uncertainties, she'd experienced that. The trouble certainly hadn't disappeared, but she'd survived it.

"They'd be crazy if they did." Mark brushed his fingers against her cheek. "I believe you."

She needed more than that. His weak assurance didn't touch her fear. "Please take me back."

eighteen

The next morning, Evelyn received orders to report back to work. Without a word, the navy cleared her of any suspicion. Unfortunately, no one said anything to the other WAVES. She felt the lingering uncertainty from many of them as she walked around Building 26 and Sugar Camp. Her roommates and a few others remained unchanged—mainly the women she'd spent time with and knew well.

After a silent weekend, Evelyn found Lt. Meyers Monday morning.

The woman sat behind her desk in her closet-sized office. "What can I do for you, Ensign Happ?"

"I'm requesting reassignment to Washington DC."

Lt. Meyers considered her a moment. "The cause?"

"The navy has cast enough suspicion on me that my fellow WAVES distrust me. I need a new forum. Surely that's where Admiral Meader intended to send me months ago."

The officer reached for a pad of paper and scribbled a note. "I can't make any promises but will inquire with Washington. See if they can use your skills with the Bombes there."

"Thank you."

It was all she could expect. Now she'd have to wait.

❧

Evelyn trudged into Adam's room. Mark hated knowing that he'd inadvertently started the process that led to her questioning. She'd relaxed on Sunday, but back in Building 26 with all eyes on her, she'd retreated.

Any time he tried to engage her, pain hid in her eyes. While he didn't point Meader and the rest toward her, he should have done more to shift their focus faster. With the disappearance of Anthony from the building, he assumed the navy had decided Anthony was the only one involved.

Yet each day, Evelyn seemed to slip away from him. Not that she said anything, but he sensed a subtle distance. By Wednesday, he needed to say something. During the morning break, he ran to the cafeteria and purchased two cups of coffee. Returning to the room, he saw her disappearing around a corner in the hallway. He adjusted course and followed.

She pushed open a side door and stepped outside. A moment later, he joined her.

"Evelyn?"

She started and turned to him. Her lips thinned.

"I brought coffee." He handed it to her, a weak offering.

"Thank you."

The cold air cut through him, enough to make him wish he'd grabbed his jacket before following her. She shivered, then took a swallow. Mark let the silence lengthen between them, waiting for her.

"I have the opportunity to join the next group of Bombes in DC."

His jaw dropped. "Why leave?"

"Life's been awkward since Meader put me on leave. Even coming back hasn't helped."

"Give it more time." She couldn't leave. Not now. Not when he loved her.

She turned, her gaze searching his face. He wanted to pull her toward him, tell her he'd be the man she needed. If only she'd stay. She swallowed, and her expression closed.

"I have to let them know today."

That soon? He needed time to change her mind. "Don't go."

"Why? I have family in DC."

"Family that doesn't care about you." She bristled at his words. "When was the last time you heard from them?"

She shrugged. "It doesn't matter."

"Yes, it does. You can't run away on the excuse of family. If they cared, they'd be in touch with you."

"If I go to DC, I'll have anonymity again. Nobody there will know about what happened here."

"Then stay so we can see what develops between us."

"More than friendship?" Her gaze searched his as if to see his soul more clearly.

"Yes." He nodded so hard his coffee sloshed. He switched the cup to his other hand and shook the hot liquid off.

"I can't do that right now." She stepped back. "A kiss isn't enough to let me think we could have more. I want forever with someone I can trust. Maybe the distance will show us if this is real."

"Forever? That's a really long time." Mark tried to infuse humor into his voice. Based on her expression, he failed.

"Yes."

Mark didn't know what to say. He wanted to believe she sensed the possibilities that existed between them. If she didn't by now, he couldn't force her to see how much he cared. He stiffened his back even as part of him whispered he would regret his stubbornness. "If you don't understand me yet, there's not much more I can say or do."

Shadows filled her eyes. He hadn't realized how much blame she pinned on him. Now that he saw things through her eyes, maybe she was right.

"I'm heading home. My family will love having me back even if I'm still in uniform."

She turned to walk away, and Mark wondered if by letting her leave, he also let the best thing in his life walk away. He stood up, and placed a hand on her arm, but she gently shook it off.

"Good-bye, Mark."

❧

Evelyn hurried to Lt. Meyers's office. She had to escape Mark and the realization friendship wasn't enough. Not now.

No, she needed to get away. Start over in DC. Avoid the rumors and escape Mark. Even if she'd be more alone there than here. Her parents would be too busy to notice she'd returned, and she'd have to start from scratch with friends in the WAVES. But she'd do it.

"Lt. Meyers, I accept the reassignment."

The lieutenant's eyes looked tired. "Don't thank me yet. The Bombes leave tonight, so you leave at seven."

"Tonight?" So soon? She had so much to do if she had to leave in a few hours.

"Yes. I suggest you head to Sugar Camp and pack. I'll send a sailor at six to assist you with your bags."

"Thank you."

"You're welcome." Lt. Meyers studied her a moment. "I hope you put this event behind you and move forward. You've been an asset to this program."

Evelyn nodded. A change of scenery. That's all she needed. Once again, she could find significance in her contribution to the war effort—somewhere other than in Dayton. "Where should I report?"

"Go with the Bombes to the Naval Communications Annex. From there, they should have an assignment for you. You may have to find your own housing."

That would be the easy part since she could live at home for a bit.

Lt. Meyers handed her an envelope. "This contains your orders. Good luck, Ensign."

Evelyn saluted and backed out of the room. Once in the hallway, she shut the door and hurried to Adam's room. Mark looked up from his work when she entered, but she grabbed her hat and purse before he could say anything.

At John's questioning glance, she smiled. "I've been reassigned to DC. I leave tonight." She ignored the way Mark jolted at the words. "It's been an honor to work with you on this project." Evelyn nodded to the men and slipped from the room.

She needed this break. No sense dragging it out. Mark wouldn't offer what she needed to keep her here. And with her orders firmly in hand, she no longer had the option to stay.

Once she reached Sugar Camp, she hurried to her cabin. Who would have thought the small room would feel like home after six short months? As she packed, her gaze trailed to the drooping sunflowers. Why couldn't Mark put into words what the flowers conveyed? Mark wouldn't send flowers to just anybody. It wasn't his style. And she would not allow herself to believe what she wanted about another man. No, he'd have to say he loved her, ask her to stay, before she could do anything differently.

*

It didn't take Evelyn long to pack her uniforms, books, and minimal personal items. She settled at the small desk to write quick notes to her roommates. Viv wouldn't understand her sudden departure, but that couldn't be helped. Orders were orders.

Next, she wrote a quick letter to Marjorie. Tears slipped down her cheeks at the thought of leaving this woman who had ushered her to her heavenly Father. She had a lifetime of growing to do, all possible because Marjorie took the time to answer each of her questions.

One sheet of paper remained.

She stared at it. It begged to be filled with a message to Mark. What should she say?

When she placed the pen on the paper, the words flowed.

*

By Friday evening, Mark couldn't wait to get away from work. The week had dragged, Evelyn's reassignment setting him on his heels. He'd wanted to escape work, but problems had developed that required the engineers to put in long shifts. As they'd wrestled with the latest kinks, he'd missed Evelyn. They needed her different approach to problems.

Fortunately, Kat kept the dinner conversations going laced with all the events of her senior year. And Cassandra and Art Jr. distracted his mom. She hadn't asked about Evelyn yet. Made him wonder if somehow she already knew.

It didn't matter.

The only thing that mattered was Evelyn had left, and he'd let her. What a fool!

Her absence emphasized what her presence had added to his life. Yes, she was beautiful. But her mind intrigued him. And her growing love for the Lord humbled and challenged him.

He stopped in the middle of the sidewalk.

That's what he should have done all along. Asked the Lord whether Evelyn might be the one for him.

He needed to pray. Turn her and any possibility of a relationship with her over to the Father. *Lord, be with Evelyn as she works in a new place. Give her favor and wisdom. Father, I need Your wisdom, too. She's an amazing woman. I'll confess I'm only now realizing how amazing. Help me discern whether to let go or pursue her.*

Peace eased down on him. He might not have clearer direction yet, but he'd turned her over to the One who loved her most.

When he entered the house, he sifted through the mail piled on the hall table. He found one envelope addressed to him in feminine handwriting that looked like Evelyn's. From Dayton. He ripped the envelope and pulled out a single sheet of paper.

He looked for the signature first. Evelyn. Slipping the sheet in his pocket, he headed upstairs. This letter would be read in the privacy of his room.

Once in his room, he pulled out the letter and sank to his bed. Unfolding it, he read it, then read it again:

Mark,

I hope you understand why I left. I couldn't stay, not with the rumors about me and the lack of a promise from you. I will always treasure your friendship. And wish you the best. If you ever need to find me, I'll be at the Naval Communications Annex in Washington. My time in Dayton was richer for knowing you.

Yours forever,
Evelyn

He read it again, and a flicker of hope ignited. The letter wasn't what he'd hoped, yet she'd made it clear she wouldn't be the first to declare her feelings. She might not have said the words outright, but she'd given hints. She was his forever.

He needed to make those words come true.

❧

Evelyn's first days in DC settled into a routine, with Mark never far from her thoughts. Part of her wanted to believe he meant what he'd said. That he could really love her. Each time she tried to believe, her heart reminded her of another man who had said those words only to leave her days before their wedding. If she couldn't trust Paul's words, could she trust Mark?

In so many ways the two were opposites. Mark believed in God; Paul believed in himself. Mark worked tirelessly; Paul enjoyed the privileged life. Yet both confessed their love for her. And Paul had proven untrustworthy.

She wanted to believe Mark. But could she force her heart to accept what her head knew? Mark would never hurt her the way Paul had.

Work provided a refuge. The Naval Communications Annex near Tenley Square was different from Sugar Camp and Building 26. Dozens of Bombes ran around the clock, filling the rooms with heat and an amazing volume of noise. Her superiors quickly assigned her to the group charged with keeping the machines running. The design developed at NCR worked. The machines endured almost constant use at incredible speeds. If only the WAVES who worked in the rooms could withstand the heat as well.

The first time Evelyn noticed the salt dispensers next to the water fountain she hadn't known what to think until a colleague explained the need to consume extra salt and water. After a week, Evelyn knew all too well the importance of having enough salt and fluids in her body. Without them, the heat made her faint. Fortunately, she'd left the swooning to others.

The loneliness she felt now surprised her. Even though she lived with other WAVES on the converted grounds of Mount Vernon Seminary for Girls, she struggled to build the camaraderie she'd left in Dayton. Hundreds of people surrounded her during her shifts. And when she was off duty, she shared a room with other enlisted WAVES. Instead of the rustic feel of Sugar Camp, the annex felt like a prison circled with barbed wire and guards.

What she wouldn't give to have Viv, Lonnie, or Mary Ellen here. Though her family was nearby, they were too busy to do more than invite her to the occasional fundraiser. She hadn't expected more, but it still stung. Through it all, God never left her. She sensed His presence as she read His Word and prayed. She came to depend on the assurance He was with her.

Even so, Evelyn needed to connect with her colleagues. Her first weekend in DC, she joined a group going horseback riding in Rock Creek Park. A new roommate, Allison, chattered during the quick walk to the rendezvous point.

"Just wait until you see the park! It's like escaping completely from the city." The gal had her dark hair pulled out of her face with a scarf. She wore dungarees with a heavy jacket, boots, and gloves. "The group of us try to get away once a week for riding. As close as it is, you'd think we'd manage more often."

Evelyn tried to keep up with Allison's high-speed words and steps. "I love the park." Her parents' house wasn't far from it. "I haven't ridden much, though I've always thought it would be fun."

"Tell Pierre you need a gentle horse. He takes good care of us WAVES."

A blond gal nodded. "And wait till you see him. He looks like a movie star."

"Instead, he takes care of horses." A woman shook her head. "I don't mind, though, because we get to admire him when we're at the park."

Evelyn laughed. "And to think, I thought this was about the horses."

"Oh, that's an attraction, only a distant second." Allison tucked her arm through Evelyn's.

"Wait until you see him." The blond heaved a dramatic sigh.

"I doubt he compares to my man." Evelyn stopped walking. *Her man?* What was she thinking? She tucked her head and prayed. As much as she might want Mark to be hers, until he saw her as special, nothing would come of it. And she didn't need these gals to start questioning her about Mark. Their relationship was simply too complicated to explain. Colleagues? Friends? Sweethearts? If only they had bridged to sweethearts.

Allison stopped to watch Evelyn carefully. "You have a story to tell, my dear."

Heat she couldn't blame on the Bombes seared Evelyn's cheeks.

Allison leaned closer to Evelyn and faux-whispered in her ear, "Tell me all about it when we're alone."

The group giggled and picked up their pace. By the time they reached the park, Evelyn was more than ready to let a horse carry her. After Pierre matched them with horses, Evelyn hung back. Her horse seemed gentle, but she didn't want the others to watch while she found her balance. The gentle bump of the horse's starts and stops almost unseated her a couple of times. As she became comfortable with the horse's motion, her thoughts returned to Mark. This was the type of activity they could enjoy together.

And if she ever returned to Dayton, maybe they'd try.

nineteen

Six weeks since Evelyn Happ had disappeared from his life.

Mark rolled over in bed. Each day felt like a month. The knowledge settled deeper into his gut. Evelyn was the woman for him.

Did she feel the same way?

The only failsafe method: Ask her. And that he couldn't leave to a letter. No matter how he tried to pen the words, they never mirrored the depth of what he felt.

No, this was a conversation that required face-to-face communication. Her response was an unknown factor, so she needed to read his face, view the depth of his love without a filter of distance between them. And he needed to see her reaction without the delay of time and the uncertainty of written words.

How could he get to DC? The navy hadn't let up on Desch, who hadn't let up on him. As long as the war raged, work would continue unabated at NCR and Building 26.

He had to know now if Evelyn loved him, if there was any way he could capture her heart.

Mark felt trapped in his room. The twin bed that he'd slept in for twenty-some years now confined. The stacks of *National Geographic*s he'd bought over the years teetered around him like piles of junk. Would Evelyn make room for them or toss them? He picked up the top issue and flipped the pages. He stopped at the photo of WAVES in formation in Algiers. The image of the women marching smartly in their crisp uniforms and hats made him ache to see Evelyn.

Enough.

He had to do something before he turned into a sniveling, romantic mess. He should address this logically.

He stomped out of his room and downstairs. Living in a house overrun with women and adolescents had worn him down. But he needed a strong dose of his mother's wisdom. She knew Evelyn well and might have insight he needed.

Gales of laughter—the feminine, over-the-top kind—trickled down the hallway through the closed kitchen door. Mark stopped outside it and considered retreating upstairs. He could always talk to Mom later. But the tightness in his chest every time he thought of Evelyn—and when didn't he?—forced him through the door. Besides, as overrun as the house was, it could be a long time before he caught Mom without a crowd. Art Jr. or Cassandra would surely be curled up next to her, or Kat would demand her time with the latest high school crisis.

Nope, better to do it now.

And time to consider getting a place of his own, once the war ended and housing eased up again.

The door pushed out, and Art screeched as he collided with Mark's legs. Mark took a step back and grabbed the child. "What's up, squirt?"

"Tired of girls." Art Jr.'s green eyes rounded and his mouth puckered like he'd bitten into something nasty.

Mark laughed at the child's words. "Me, too, buddy."

"Hey." Kat held the door open, hand cocked on her hip. "I thought Mama always told you to say kind words or keep silent."

"I didn't say it exactly like that, Kat." Mom peeked around the door, flour dusting her cheeks and hair. Baking turned into a contact sport.

"My most humble apologies." Mark pulled Art up on his shoulder, then swooped down into a full bow. Art giggled, a sound that made Mark smile. He righted himself and set Art back on the floor. "Off with you, Master Art."

Art grinned and tore down the hall and up the stairs, his small feet making an amazing racket.

Kat wrinkled her nose at Mark, then yelled into the kitchen,

"Come on, Cassandra. I'll help you with your math homework. I know it's beyond Josie."

The mischievous glint in her eyes had Mark struggling to hold his frown. "What was that about only saying nice things?"

"That applies to everyone else, of course." She shrugged her shoulders and made an angelic face before waltzing into the dining room, Cassandra following. The girl had latched onto Kat from the moment she returned home. Probably did her good to have someone like Kat to follow around as she worked her way through American schools. Nothing affected that kid's rosy take on life.

Only Josie remained in the kitchen with Mom. As Mark entered the room, the scents of tomato and spices made his stomach rumble. "Josie, could I have a few moments with Mom?"

Josie looked up from the pile of potatoes and peels in front of her. "I'm almost done."

Mom turned from the stove to look at Mark. Something in his expression must have caught her attention. "We'll go down to the basement. I could use your help bringing some wood up. A fire in the fireplace will be perfect tonight."

"All right." Mark followed her down the wooden stairs, the clack of her heels against them sounding like the rapport of guns.

"What's bothering you, Mark?"

"I need your advice."

Mom sat on the edge of a sheet-covered chair. "Of course."

"What do you think of Evelyn?"

"You know I love her. She's a dear friend."

Mark rubbed his hands over his hair. Time to get another haircut, especially if he visited Evelyn. "I mean more than that." His tongue felt twisted into knots and refused to cooperate. "I. . .I miss her."

A soft light filled Mom's eyes. "I know."

"What do you think I should do?"

"Have you prayed?"

"It seems I've done nothing but pray. Ever since she left. Even before."

"And what is God telling you?"

Mark slumped against the wall. "That's the problem. No matter how I ask, silence is all I hear."

Mom reached out and stroked his arm, much as she had when he'd been a frustrated boy. "I've rarely heard God speak in an audible way. Often it's more of an impression. A certainty that something is right. A peace that doesn't make sense but is unshakeable. A knowing a certain path is the one for me."

Mark nodded. He could relate. "I get that kind of certainty when I pray about Evelyn and me."

"Is there anything about your relationship that doesn't line up with scripture?"

"Now that she's a Christian? No."

"If I hadn't walked her through that process, I might caution giving it more time." Mom held up a hand to prevent his protest. "But I've watched her closely, Mark. Her faith may be new, but she's committed and growing."

"But what do I do?"

Mom stood. "That, I can't tell you. You're an adult and have to make these decisions yourself. But I will pray for you. I have no reservations about you and Evelyn. She is a wonderful young woman. One I would be proud to add to our family." A teasing smile tipped her cheeks. "Though that would only make you more outnumbered."

"It would be worth it." *So very worth it.*

Mom must have read his mind because she laughed. "Enough. Your Dad and I will pray. You do the same and act as God leads. We'll support you either way. Now get some of that wood and take it upstairs before one of the others comes looking for us."

Long after their conversation, Mark's mind continued to spin. His mom would bless their marriage. A similar talk with Dad told Mark his parents agreed on the subject. Now to pray some more. Make sure God approved.

Evelyn tucked her chin and shrugged her collar, trying to burrow deeper into her coat against a sharp wind. The weather forecast had made snow a possibility, and based on the clouds, it would fall sooner rather than later. She hurried to the navy vehicle, the satchel with communications strapped across her chest. She'd gladly accepted the task of delivering the missives to the Pentagon.

Her days had fallen into a pattern. The rotation of working three different eight-hour shifts over five days before getting two days off left her internal clock confused. Her body never knew when to sleep and when to wake up. Someone in the navy had decided the schedule was a good idea, but she seriously doubted that person ever worked the rotation.

She steered the car through security, exiting the annex before taking Nebraska Avenue to Wisconsin and eventually driving across the Arlington Memorial Bridge into Virginia. Evelyn finally worked her way through several layers of Pentagon security. Acres of cars stood between her and the five-sided building. Rumor had it one could walk more than seventeen miles in the Pentagon's complex levels and layers. The building was a vast improvement over the former marshes and swamps, but big enough to leave her overwhelmed.

She parked her car, grabbed the satchel, and hiked across the parking lots and up the stairs. Finally, she reached the building and worked her way through more security.

"Ensign Happ." A sailor appeared in front of her, good-looking enough to appear in recruiting materials. He saluted with a flourish. "Petty Officer Charles Stuart at your service. I'm to escort you."

"Thank you."

"Follow me."

His formal manner eased as they headed deeper into the bowels of the building. After leading her around another corner, he stopped and winked. "Join me for a cup of coffee after you drop off the communications?"

Evelyn felt conspicuous while a stream of military and civilians passed them. She cleared her throat. "I'm expected back promptly."

He lazed a grin in her direction. "Everyone has to take a break."

"I'll take mine after the war, thank you." Evelyn tightened her shoulder blades and tried to send him a strong not-interested signal. Yes, this man could turn the head of any woman, but in the few minutes they'd interacted, he'd proved he was no Mark. She took off down the hallway. "This way?"

His laughter chased her, and after twenty yards, he caught up with her. "All right. You've made your point. I'll get you to the office and back out. And whoever this guy is, he's very lucky."

"What makes you think there's someone?"

"Most gals are more than happy to take a break with me. And the annex won't miss fifteen minutes. So something else holds you back. Another guy."

Evelyn smiled, awkward at the thought this man—a stranger—could read her so easily.

Yet emptiness weighed against her. It was too late to dwell on how much Mark meant to her.

"Here we are." Petty Officer Stuart grinned. "I'll come back in five minutes to lead you out of this maze."

"Thank you." Evelyn turned over the satchel to the appropriate person and retrieved a different case. When he returned, Petty Officer Stuart tried to carry it for her, but she refused. If anything happened to that bag, the navy would have her head, not his.

"Are you sure you won't break for a few minutes with me?" He turned the full force of his blue eyes on her. Charm oozed from him.

"No. Thank you for your assistance." She nodded to him and headed toward the main doors before he could waylay her again.

Yes, he was handsome and appealing, but he wasn't Mark. And Mark was the only man she wanted.

twenty

"Mr. Miller," Desch blustered his morning greeting. "You're on the next train to DC."

DC? NCR would send him to work with Evelyn? Mark stood straighter and nodded. "Of course, sir." He turned to head out of the room, ready to pack his bag. A throat cleared, and he turned back around. "Yes?"

"Aren't you forgetting something?"

John snorted. "Of course not. He's remembering that's where his girl is."

"Yeah. Yeah." Desch's frown caused Mark to clear his throat. "My assignment in Washington?"

"There's a new problem with the Bombes. Cable and phone communication isn't remedying it, so I want someone there. Fix it, and you'll be back."

His excitement nose-dived. What if he didn't want to come back? Christmas was a week away, and he could imagine a great gift for a certain WAVES.

"Well?" Desch stared at him, tapping his foot impatiently.

"Yes, sir. I'll catch the next train."

"You're booked. Collect your tickets from my assistant."

Mark turned and hurried from the room. In short order, he had his ticket and his packed bag and had hailed a cab to the station.

Once he climbed aboard the train bound for Washington, nervous energy made it difficult to sit still. He considered calling ahead, but had no way to reach Evelyn. She'd been conspicuously silent. He hadn't received a letter since the one she'd mailed before leaving. He couldn't say for sure where she lived.

He loved her. Totally, completely, couldn't imagine anyone

159

else in his life. He'd never felt this way before, even with Paige. His stomach roiled at the idea he might spend days in Washington DC at the Naval Communications Annex and not run into Evelyn.

Father, help me find her. I need to talk to her, see if she feels the same way. And thanks for the opportunity to go.

The train crawled east across the landscape. The countryside slid past the windows but never fast enough. He hunkered down with a stack of magazines but couldn't focus on any article. Instead, he imagined how a reunion scene with Evelyn would play out. The images in his mind ranged from her jumping into his arms to her walking away on the arm of another man.

He wanted to define their relationship, and he had to trust God with it. He certainly couldn't control the outcome.

A day later, the train finally pulled into Union Station. Mark joined the rush of people pushing to exit the train. His only instruction had been to report to the Naval Communications Annex. He wandered around the station until he found a taxi stand by the Columbus Statue in front. The mob of people and crush of vehicles was so different from Dayton. Dayton wasn't a small town, but DC had an energy and drive that Mark identified immediately. It reminded him of Evelyn. No wonder Evelyn pushed the way she did. Anyone who grew up here would do that.

The cab had to release him on Nebraska Avenue, and Mark walked to the fence guarding the annex. The sun's reflection glinted off the barbed wire and marines' guns.

"Can I help you, sir?" One marine stepped from the guard station, while others remained focused on the traffic outside the compound.

"I'm here from Dayton."

The marine stiffened his stance, his bulk pushing Mark back a pace. "You can't proceed without proper authorization."

"I have my orders right here." Mark reached inside his coat, but stopped when the marine pointed his gun at his chest.

"Whoa. Don't shoot. I'm reaching for my orders."

The man looked askance at him. Orders without uniform must not register. "Point the pocket out. I'll retrieve them."

Mark put his hands in the air and nodded. "Inside left pocket."

The marine stepped forward, reached inside Mark's coat, and pulled out the envelope. Mark put his hands down but watched closely. He hadn't gotten this close to Evelyn to get shot.

"Don't move." The man reentered the guard station and placed a call as he watched Mark.

Mark stared at the two other guards. They appeared more annoyed at his presence than anything else, but he couldn't relax and learn he'd misread them. The marine returned, his frown etched more deeply into his skin.

"What is the nature of your business here?"

How should he answer? He couldn't divulge much without revealing the project. The marines might know the nature of the machines and the work they did. Then again, they might not have a clue what they protected. He had to get into one of the red brick buildings before him where he'd find Evelyn.

"If I told you, the navy officers in Dayton would have me shot. Either you've confirmed my orders or haven't. If you have, let me pass."

The marine stared him down, then waved him through. Mark kept his back stiff until he got beyond the guards. He looked around. Almost a dozen buildings dotted the landscape in front of him. Which was the one he needed?

"Mr. Miller?"

Mark heard the voice and hesitated before turning back to the guard shack. "An escort will take you to your building and get you any passes you need."

Mark nodded and turned around to wait. People walked across the campus in front of him, all with the determined strides of having work to do. He felt out of place as he idled with a briefcase and bag. A short man hurried across the area toward him.

"Mr. Miller?"

"Yes."

"Follow me." His guide double-timed it toward a building Mark could barely see. "We're glad you've arrived. The machines are falling to pieces again for no apparent reason. Ensign Happ suggested someone from your team at NCR could identify the problem."

At Evelyn's name, Mark tuned everything else out. He'd see her. Soon.

❧

The Bombes whirred around Evelyn. Even though it was the middle of December, the machines generated enough heat to keep the room stifling. The constant noise sounded better than the sudden quiet that had almost deafened her a few days ago.

One by one, the machines had broken down. The silence had been eerie.

The noise that replaced it never sounded so good.

The WAVES had jerry-built a system that worked. But she'd feel better when someone from NCR approved it. It should be harder than brushing the rotors off carefully to remove any shavings or other debris from the faces.

The more she worked with the machines, the more delicate they became. Keeping them operating was enough to drive a girl crazy. Evelyn wiped her forehead off with a damp handkerchief.

A gentle touch on her arm caused her to gasp, then spin around. "Mark!" She jumped into his arms before she could think.

A twinkle filled his eyes. "I take it you missed me."

The gals around them laughed.

She ducked her head against his shoulder, enjoying the strength and feel of him, and pulled back as a couple of whistles added to the noise. "Back to work, ladies."

Mark held her a moment longer, then eased away. She drank in the sight of him and enjoyed watching him do the same with her. He grinned. "Maybe I should walk out and come back in. Would I get another welcome like that?"

Annoying heat filled her face. He rubbed a finger across her cheek in a caress she leaned into. "I've missed you, Evelyn."

"And I you." She looked about the room. Everyone pretended to be focused on anything but them, but she knew it was an act. In no time, word of her welcome would float all over the building. "Let's talk later."

Mark glanced around and straightened. "Of course." *Sorry,* he mouthed. He tucked his bag and briefcase against the wall. "How can I help?"

"I hoped NCR would send you. I think I've reached a solution—at least a tentative one—but would like your take." She walked him around the machines and explained what had happened. "So we've given the rotors an extra brushing with that brush Mr. Desch recommended. I think the maintenance lightened a bit after the machines were here awhile. Routine and all that."

"Are the other WAVES careful when changing the rotors?"

"Yes. There are the occasional near misses when one flies off and lodges in the floor or a wall, but so far, no one's been hurt."

Mark stopped and watched a Bombe run. "It may be time for refresher training. Reinforce how dangerous these machines are. How delicate to operate."

"You're the expert."

"You are, too."

"No, I'm another WAVES who's telling them what to do—one who hasn't been here long, at that." Evelyn wanted to retrieve the words and the edge they contained. Mark eyed her with concern. "Never mind. We'll discuss that later. You need to get settled."

"Have dinner with me tonight."

Evelyn considered him a moment. How she'd longed for more time with him. "I'd like that."

"Great. If you show me where I'm staying, I'll figure out how to pick you up."

Laughter bubbled up from inside her. "I don't think you need to worry about that. We'll walk somewhere close. Maybe even stay at the cafeteria since that's our usual pattern."

"Oh no. You've been gone for weeks—"

"Six."

"It felt longer. We're going somewhere we can celebrate being together again."

It sounded like he'd missed her almost as much as she'd missed him. Maybe that old saying about absence making the heart grow fonder wasn't crazy. She wouldn't argue with him if he wanted to spoil her. No, she'd enjoy every moment until he returned to Dayton. And she refused to let that impending reality destroy her enjoyment of this moment.

⁂

Several hours later, Mark wondered if he'd been crazy to come. His quarters were with the commander, who lived in the old headmistress's home. A hotel would be less awkward, though this allowed the navy to monitor his comings and goings efficiently.

At least he had his passes and a pillow to lay his head on. Evelyn had told him hotel rooms were hard to come by in the war-inflated town.

Getting time alone with Evelyn might prove more difficult. He'd already had to send a message canceling his plans with her when the commander had insisted on hearing his initial thoughts and how he wanted to proceed. Would she understand he didn't have a choice about canceling and realize how disappointed he was? He came to spend time with her, not some officer.

All he wanted to do was talk with Evelyn.

A knock sounded on his door. Mark sat up on the twin bed. "Yes?"

"Time for dinner, Mr. Miller."

"Thank you."

Mark pulled his shoes out from under the bed and put them on. With a quick look in the mirror, he headed out the door and down the stairs.

A sailor waited at the bottom of the stairs. "Follow me."

Soon he sat at the table with a handful of other men, the commander, and his wife. The conversation flowed around him, until the woman leaned toward him. "Mr. Miller, do you have special plans while you're here?"

"No, ma'am. Perform my job and return to Dayton."

"If you're here long enough, I invite you to accompany us to the White House on Christmas Eve for the Christmas tree lighting and program. It's usually quite the event. Surely you'll stay two more days."

"Thank you."

She turned to the man on her other side, and Mark took another bite of roast. As he did, a plan formed in his mind. It might work, and if it did, he'd be the happiest of men. It would take a bit of doing, though. As Mark took another bite, he mulled the developing plan. He had to try. Two days until Christmas Eve. Would it be long enough to find a ring and pull it together?

twenty-one

Evelyn stifled the disappointment that zinged through her as another day closed. Mark had worked closely with her, but other than a quick apology for canceling their dinner plans the night before had said nothing about rescheduling.

Maybe the magic of their reunion had already died.

She caught him watching her and smiled. No, the connection had only intensified.

In a few minutes, her shift would end, and unless he said something, she'd leave. Without him. She'd gladly get away from the curious looks from the gals in the room—they all continued to watch her as if waiting for the next installment in a drama. But it also meant leaving Mark. What should she do? The Bombes had worked perfectly after her recommended adjustments. Maybe that would shorten Mark's stay, and he planned to go home for Christmas. If so, he'd leave in the morning. He'd have no reason to stay—other than her.

"Why the heavy sigh?" Mark studied her.

"Who, me?" Evelyn looked around the room. "I didn't realize I sighed."

"Do you have plans tomorrow night?"

"It's Christmas Eve, Mark. I'll have dinner with my parents. You're welcome to join us, but you'll be on your way home, right? Back with your family?"

"I'd like to stay here. Spend it with you. If that's all right."

Evelyn bit her lip. She wanted nothing more but didn't want to be his charity case. "I'm sure your mom will want you home."

He paled as if she'd said something that pained him. "She knew when I left I likely wouldn't be back in time. Do you want me out of here?" Mark edged closer until Evelyn could smell his musky aftershave. "I want to spend the time with you."

"I would like that." A smile curved her mouth. "Very much."

"Great. Bundle up tomorrow."

"Why?"

"We'll go to the Christmas tree celebration at the White House."

"That's perfect. We'll have time afterward for dinner and a Christmas Eve service with my family."

He looked like a kid in the middle of planning a surprise.

She leaned close and whispered in his ear. "Do we have to wait until tomorrow?" Had she been that forward? Not something she'd normally say, but she couldn't let him leave DC without knowing she wanted to spend time with him.

After all, she couldn't tell him anything meaningful while surrounded by women waiting to spread the information through the gossip mills. No, she needed time alone with him, out of sight of the others. They could talk, and maybe she'd learn if he felt the same way she did.

❧

A tinge of relief flushed Mark at the hint of panic flecking Evelyn's eyes. It pained him to see the edge of desperation, but it also made him think she would accept when he asked her to marry him tomorrow.

This woman he loved remained an enigma in so many ways. They'd known each other a number of months, but the separation had left him wondering. When she hadn't communicated with him at all, he'd wondered if she'd washed her hands of him. Now he believed she mirrored his feelings.

"Dinner tonight? I don't think the commander expects me." He could make time for Evelyn and still pull his plans together.

A radiant smile curved her lips. She looked around the room then leaned back in. "We might even be able to sneak out now."

Mark laughed and shook his head. "Oh no. We'll work hard and finish our shift. Then we'll get away."

"All right." She slipped away, walking among the Bombes. He watched her glide between them, each step as graceful as a dance.

He needed to follow his own advice. He turned to the pages in front of him, reviewing Evelyn's detailed notes of what had happened as the Bombes broke down and how she'd responded. Her work impressed him. She'd done everything he would have done and appeared to have successfully resolved the problem. He couldn't think of anything to add. Desch would be glad for the report. One more crisis averted through hard work, engineering prowess, and common sense.

As soon as their shift ended, Mark helped Evelyn into her coat and guided her down the hall. "Where do you recommend?"

"Some of the WAVES speak highly of a place about a mile from here."

"Want a taxi or exercise?"

Evelyn grinned at him. "A walk takes more time."

"Walk it is." Mark turned up his collar and edged her against him. After they discussed a training program he could do after Christmas, he filled her in on his family, telling her all about the chaos in his parents' home. She laughed as he spun story after story starring Art Jr. The kid was an active, engaging three-year-old. Mark couldn't wait to have one of his own. He tucked Evelyn closer, shielding her from the breeze. "So how's your time here been?"

She kicked at a clod of snow on the sidewalk. "I never thought I'd say this, but I miss Dayton."

"The city?"

"I don't know how much of it is the city. I probably miss the people more. You, your family, my roommates, and fellow WAVES. I can't believe how eager I was to leave because now I'd like nothing more than to return."

"Would the WAVES let you?" Mark hadn't thought about that angle. Maybe he'd need to move to DC.

"I haven't asked. I may not have any choice. If the navy

thinks I'm more valuable here, this is where I'm stuck."

"That sounds bleak."

"It's not all bad." She sighed, her breath frosting in the air. "I've enjoyed being back in the city, seeing my parents a couple of times."

Light flooded the little diner she indicated. The food was good, the service brusque in an East Coast kind of way that reminded him of Boston. But the companionship with Evelyn made the night. He escorted her to her dormitory at the close of the evening. Her nose and cheeks were tinged with red, courtesy of the cold.

"See you in the morning, Evelyn."

She leaned toward him, lips parted. He wanted to kiss her with every fiber of his being, but he stepped back. Not tonight. Not until they had a promise.

⁓

Evelyn shifted on the hard bed. The walk and dinner with Mark had been magical. Such simple things, but the time with him had filled her heart.

The next day passed in a blur. It might be Christmas Eve, but the war hadn't slowed. The last holdouts of the Warsaw Ghetto had been wiped out, the push into Italy had stalled, and action was prevalent on the Pacific front. She had to keep the Bombes operating. Any sliver of a broken code could make a difference.

Maybe someday she'd know how much of a difference.

As time raced toward the end of her shift, she found it harder to focus. Her thoughts turned to Mark. It would be fun to wow him with a dress fit for Christmas Eve festivities and services. Instead, she'd wear a fresh WAVES suit. Again.

"I'll pick you up at your dormitory in twenty minutes." Mark bounced on his heels as he talked with the same pent-up energy of his nephew.

"See you then." Evelyn let Mark hold her coat as she shrugged into it. She'd barely have time to freshen up.

A tingle of excitement coursed through her. Tonight, she'd

celebrate the birth of her Savior with the man she loved. Tears filled her eyes at the thought. Her first Christmas after acknowledging Christ as her Savior. She couldn't wait to attend a Christmas Eve service and participate with eyes newly opened to the full significance. Emmanuel. God with us.

æ

Mark slipped the small, square box into his coat pocket. It seemed to grow in size and bulk as it hid there. He played with its velvet edges as he walked across the annex to get Evelyn. The cab would meet them at the gate in five minutes.

Evelyn must have seen him walk up because she hurried out. He pulled her into a hug.

"Hello, beautiful."

"Hi." She eased back, and the lights reflected in her eyes.

"I wish I had Cinderella's coach for you. Instead, our cab should arrive in a few moments." He led her down the steps and along the sidewalk.

Evelyn tugged on his arm. "If you're looking for the front gate, we go this direction."

"Thanks." He shrugged. "Should have known I'd get turned around."

A cab idled at the curb when they reached the gate. He helped her in and gave the cabby the address: "1600 Pennsylvania Avenue."

Once they reached the White House, they followed a stream of people through the southwest gate onto the grounds. A large spruce of some sort had been decorated with hundreds of ornaments sent in by the school children of DC. They walked closer, and he suddenly understood the reason for the middle-of-the-afternoon ceremony.

"No lights."

Evelyn snuggled next to him. "Yes. Security and all that."

At the sound of "Angels We Have Heard on High," they turned to see a group of WAVES on a stage. "I'm glad you're next to me and not up there. Not that you wouldn't be a great addition."

"Nice save." Her smile faltered a bit.

Mark tugged her around the Christmas tree, away from the crowd now focused on the stage.

"Where are we going?"

"I've got a surprise for you."

She bit the side of her lip as if trying to bite back a smile. "Full of surprises, aren't you?"

"One or two."

"I didn't get you anything."

Mark tilted his head as he processed her answer. "Anything?"

"A present. I didn't know you were coming. Didn't get you anything." Her words picked up speed. He needed to slow her down somehow.

Mark slid her a step away from him. Her brow quirked, and she half-stepped toward him. He backed up another step until a branch of the spruce brushed his hair. She giggled, and reached up and picked something off his shoulder. "Is this yours?"

A circle of decorated paper dangled from her fingers.

"No. Guess I should move away from the tree." He took a deep breath. This was it.

Mark eased down on one knee, not caring that it sank into a patch of snow. Evelyn gasped then covered her mouth with a gloved hand.

"What are you doing?" Tears filled her eyes, trickling down her cheeks and shimmering like crystals.

He hadn't expected her to cry. Should he continue? As cold liquid seeped through his knees, he knew he had to. He needed to know her answer.

"Evelyn Happ, I love you." He took a deep breath. "I love the way your mind works and challenges me. The way you've given your heart to the Lord and are building your relationship with Him. I love the way being with you makes me happy." He pulled the box from his pocket, opened it. Lifted it toward her. "But I hate being separated from you. Will you marry me?"

Evelyn nodded, tears coursing down her cheeks. Mark slid the ring from the box then stood. She pulled her glove off and held out her left hand. He slid the ring on her ring finger and then leaned down and kissed her. One meant to seal the birth of their future. The birth of their promise.

A Letter To Our Readers

Dear Reader:

In order that we might better contribute to your reading enjoyment, we would appreciate your taking a few minutes to respond to the following questions. We welcome your comments and read each form and letter we receive. When completed, please return to the following:

Fiction Editor
Heartsong Presents
PO Box 719
Uhrichsville, Ohio 44683

1. Did you enjoy reading *A Promise Born* by Cara C. Putman?
   ❏ Very much! I would like to see more books by this author!
   ❏ Moderately. I would have enjoyed it more if

   _____

   _____

   _____

2. Are you a member of **Heartsong Presents**? ❏ Yes ❏ No
   If no, where did you purchase this book? _____

   _____

3. How would you rate, on a scale from 1 (poor) to 5 (superior), the cover design? _____

4. On a scale from 1 (poor) to 10 (superior), please rate the following elements.

   ____ Heroine   ____ Plot
   ____ Hero   ____ Inspirational theme
   ____ Setting   ____ Secondary characters

5. These characters were special because? _____

_____

_____

6. How has this book inspired your life? _____

_____

_____

7. What settings would you like to see covered in future
Heartsong Presents books? _____

_____

_____

8. What are some inspirational themes you would like to see
treated in future books? _____

_____

_____

9. Would you be interested in reading other **Heartsong
Presents** titles? ❏ Yes   ❏ No

10. Please check your age range:
    ❏ Under 18   ❏ 18-24
    ❏ 25-34   ❏ 35-45
    ❏ 46-55   ❏ Over 55

Name _____

Occupation _____

Address _____

City, State, Zip _____

E-mail _____